Dedication

I give thanks to my Lord and Savior Jesus Christ.
May Your will and purpose be brought forth through
these works.

...and to Erica Graves

Acknowledgments

I would like to thank my family and friends for their continuous support, and Kyna Bryant for her countless hours of editorial skill on this project.

A special thanks to George Poppagoplus for his artistic skills in developing the graphic for the cover of this book.

# Contents

# TWEEDY

The front door across the street slammed so hard it startled Sis, Jerean, and Etta. The three girls charged the large living room window, carefully pulled back the thick, green-velvet curtains, and peered outside. The sky was a charcoal gray, and a steady stream of rain impaired their view. The already dim light from a single fixture hanging in the middle of the living room flickered when a series of lightning flashes lit up the entire sky.

That was the first opportunity the girls had to catch a glimpse of Tweedy jacking Mr. Jennings up by his shirt collar.

"Cut off the light," Sis whispered.

Mr. Jennings, a well-respected pillar of the community, ran a small convenience store right from his house. He was a reticent man who kept to himself.

The timid Mr. Jennings rose to the tip of his toes in an act of surrender. The heavy wool, feathered trench coat that Tweedy wore completely hid Mr. Jennings' small frame. Their conversation was mute except for Tweedy's occasional outburst of profanity.

"Cut off the light!" Sis demanded again.

Jerean pulled away from the window and snatched the hanging cord of the light.

"What happened?" she asked, repositioning herself beside Etta.

"Nothing," Etta replied. "I think he's still got him by the collar."

"It's so dark I can't see anything," Jerean mumbled. With a sharp nudge in Etta's side, Jerean insisted that she make some space for her to look.

"Are they still there?" Etta asked, turning her head slightly toward Sis for an answer.

Abruptly Sis snapped at the two of them, "If you two would shut up, maybe we could hear something." A roar of thunder, preceded by a crack of lightning, bellowed loudly across the sky. The entire street, and it seemed especially Mr. Jennings' house, was illuminated. Tweedy had thrust Mr. Jennings up against the front door. The door jarred open and Mr. Jennings went sailing across the entrance floor. Tweedy entered the house, leaving the door partially ajar.

Etta's eyebrows were as high as her hairline. "Did you see that?"

"We saw the same thing you saw!"

"Whatcha think he's doing, Sis, going in Mr. Jennings' house like that? His store is closed. He must be looking for something. Wonder what he looking for? Probably money. He might kill'im. Whatcha think, Sis? You think he gon kill'im?"

Jerean stretched her neck out from around the velvet curtain, impatiently waiting for Sis to justify Tweedy's actions.

"I think you need to shut up!" growled Sis. "Stop asking me so many questions."

"But, Sis, Jerean is right, he got to be goin' in there for something."

"Well, how do you know?" Sis asked. "Tweedy terrorizes everybody. He don't care 'bout nobody but hisself. I wouldn't be surprised if he making Mr. Jennings get him some whiskey. He ain't nothin' but a wino."

"Uh huh, winos are nice, but Tweedy is mean. He a drunk. He don't like nobody," Jerean blurted, turning her head about the room, hoping to catch a pair of eyes to stress the seriousness of her words. Sis concurred, "I heard he burned down Donna Tanner's house. Thank God they won't there. I even saw that time when he smacked Mr. Glover right in the mouth."

"Not three-hundred-pound Mr. Glover?" questioned Etta.

"Yep," Sis continued, "Mr. Glover just spoke to him while Tweedy happened to be drinking with some other fellas, so Tweedy smacked him right in the mouth, knocked all his teeth out. Then Tweedy stood proud and announced to everybody who was watching, 'Didn't y'alls mammies tell y'all never interrupt grown folks whiles they drinking?'"

Sis slid her tongue over her top teeth and felt a sense of relief that they were still there. "Po' Mr. Glover got all his teeth knocked out."

Jerean pulled back from the window, "Well, it ain't stopped Mr. Glover from eating. That man can eat a steak better with his gums than he could with his teeth. He's got false teeth, but he says he only likes to wear them on special occasions. I remember..."

Sis interrupted and ordered silence, "I think I see something."

Again the three of them peered through the window, waiting attentively for Mr. Jennings or Tweedy to reappear.

Then there came a big clap of thunder, and nervously Etta crawled from the window to the sofa. "It's dark in here," she complained. "I'm gon cut the lights on."

Sis screamed immediately, "Don't touch that light!" but Etta had already turned it on. Sis snatched the cord. "Girl, he might see that light, and what if he is doing something to Mr. Jennings? Then he'll know that we know he is over there." She paused, then made her way to the curtain to take a peek from the corner of the window.

"So, Sis, if he saw that light, he might come over here, huh?" Jerean asked, turning her head and glancing around the room.

"Listen," said Etta, "what difference does it make? Sis said he ain't doin' nothin' but stealing whiskey."

"Well, never you mind what I said befo. Just keep that light off. Next thing you know he'll be right over heah. You know Tweedy is crazy. He don't care 'bout nobody but hisself."

An expression of sympathy appeared on Etta's face, "I feel kind of sorry for him."

"Girl, are you crazy?" Sis muttered. "Tweedy don't care nothin' 'bout you. So why you gon care 'bout him?"

Jerean abandoned the window and joined in the conversation, "Etta, I saw you after church, standing on the corner with Tweedy."

In an act of defense, Etta shot back in a bitter tone, "He came over to me. I practically said nothing to him."

"What are you doing talking to Tweedy?"

Before Etta could reply, Sis was already warning her of the dangers of such a conversation.

"Girl, Tweedy would cut your tongue out of your mouth and not think twice about it. You stay away from that maniac, you hea?"

Etta's face tightened with anger, "Jerean is lying on me."

5

The look on Jerean's face changed—a look that needed no explanation, a look that closed her over-sized mouth.

"If he try to do anything to me, Daddy'll kill him." Etta released the grip of her fear and anger when she realized that her father would be home soon to protect her.

"Daddy ain't heah. And ain't no telling if he gotta work a double," Sis acknowledged angrily.

Etta stood up from the sofa, and muttered under her breath, "He ain't cutting my tongue out." Then she headed into the kitchen. Once in the kitchen, she pulled open the silverware drawer that harbored all the knives. She brandished the largest butcher knife she could find. It was an old knife. It had a worn wooden handle that was chipped and a little water-rotted, but it was big. She headed back to the living room where Jerean and Sis were paying close attention to what was or wasn't going on outside. Etta stood in the floor under the light fixture with her hand gripped tightly around the handle of the knife.

"I bet he won't cut my tongue out now," she said, surprising Sis.

Sis turned from the window to hear what Etta was talking about when a flash of lightning spotlighted the silver of the blade.

"What is that you got in your hand, Etta?"

"A butcher knife," she replied as she thrust it forward into the open air.

Etta had no intention of hurting Tweedy. She didn't want to hurt anyone, but still she rehearsed the way she would thrust the knife into his heart.

That's easy, she thought. That made her feel better. With watchful and unsure eyes, Sis shook her head, "Girl, put that knife away befo you jab yourself in the eye. Then Tweedy wouldn't have to worry about cutting your tongue out; he'd have your eye. That's all I'd need for Daddy to be down my throat asking me why this one-eyed gal is running around the house. A knife ain't to be played with."

"I thought you said you felt sorry for Tweedy," Jerean said, without turning her attention from outside.

"I do, but if he come over heah, trying to mess with me or my tongue, I'm gon gut him like a pig and feel sorry for him later."

She slashed the knife through the air again, imitating the way Tweedy would grab at the wound and later fall to the ground.

Sis laughed lightly, "You couldn't kill a fly, or see one die, as a matter of fact."

"Well," replied Etta, as she took a seat on the sofa, "maybe I never had a reason to."

Sis said nothing, but looked at Etta with inquisitive eyes to see if she really meant it. She shook her head and turned back towards the window.

After a while, Jerean broke the silence. "Happy birthday little sister," she said cheerfully.

Sis swung around, "Yeah, happy birthday."

With a light smile, Etta placed the knife on the table. "Y'all remembered. And I thought y'all forgot." The half-smile had transformed into a joyful anticipation of gifts.

"We're your sisters, girl. We know when your birthday is."

7

Now with a rather soft tone of acceptance she asked, "What did y'all get me for my birthday?"

"What you asked for," Jerean replied, as she was trying to hold in the laughter. She muzzled her mouth with both hands to prevent a loud outburst.

"But I didn't ask for nothing."

"And that's exactly what you got...nothing." They both laughed hysterically.

"Y'all ain't funny," Etta replied in a sensitive voice. "I don't care because I know Daddy gon bring me a big birthday cake."

The two of them tried to stop laughing in order to catch their breath.

Sis couldn't help it. She was laughing so hard it was causing her bladder to give. "I got to pee," she squirmed. Rising slowly to her feet and falling into another explosion of laughter, Sis passed by Etta. Etta allowed her arm to push Sis away. "It won't that funny!" Etta pulled her legs in awkwardly, hitting her knees together as if she were knock-kneed. In a fit, she lashed back at Jerean, knowing that she couldn't or wouldn't retaliate. "Shut up, Jerean," Etta insisted.

To Etta's surprise, "No!" Jerean shouted back.

A series of quick lightning flashes and a sudden clap of thunder broke the silence that had previously permeated the room.

"I get scared when it thunders," Jerean murmured.

The two of them screeched when the lightning flashed again. Etta reached for the knife and grasped the handle even tighter than before. Jerean leaned her head in closer to the window.

"I see somebody moving in the window in Mr. Jennings' house."

It was Tweedy standing at the window, in the glow of the lightning, licking the blade of a knife. Then, with the next flash of lightning, he disappeared. Jerean yanked the curtain back and sank to her knees. Fear had captured her entire body. Now she was positive that Tweedy had seen her. She turned to Etta on the sofa; her voice was shaky.

"What?" asked Etta. "Whatcha see?"

Jerean's throat was dry as the words tumbled out of her mouth, "I saw Tweedy and he had a knife."

The rain picked up tremendously, hitting hard on the tin rooftop–so hard that the sound alone was scary. The thunder roared through the sky like a thousand stampeding racehorses. Again, the sky lit up, but this time neither Mr. Jennings nor Tweedy could be seen. Quietly the two girls sat as the rain and thunder continued.

"BAM! BAM! BAM! BAM!"

Etta jerked the knife towards the front door. "Who is that?" she whispered nervously. Jerean pulled back from the window so fast that she almost bumped right into the blade of the knife.

"BAM! BAM! BAM! BAM!" The noise echoed loudly. A voice mumbled. The girls sat motionless.

A shadow darted from around the corner.

"What was that?"

"Ahhhhh!!!" they screamed.

"Don't do that, Sis."

Sis stood in the floor shivering and holding her trousers up by both hands. It was obvious that she, too, was terrified.

"Well, who is it?"

We don't know, they mouthed silently.

Sis stooped to her knees and inch-wormed her way over to the corner of the window. She pulled the curtain back slowly, closed one eye, and focused with the other until she caught the shape of the person.

"It's Tweedy," she whispered frantically to Jerean and Etta.

Tweedy staggered from one side of the porch to the other, stuttering to himself. Then he was silent, silent for what seemed like an eternity to the girls. He drifted back to the door, clutching his fist tightly until his knuckle imprints were visible. He thrust his fist into the heavy wooden door.

His heavy voice accompanied a sharp tone of rage. "Open the do'," he shouted. After waiting a moment, he drew back his large, steel-toe boot and kicked the bottom of the door. He kicked it a few more times. Several items on the wall had fallen to the floor and so did Etta and Jerean, lying completely flat, daring not to move—not even to breathe if they didn't have to.

He staggered back from the door, "I kn-n-n-now you in there. I-I ain't f-f-forgot you," yelled Tweedy.

Reaching down in the inside pocket of his trench coat, he pulled out a bottle of whiskey. He turned the bottle up and the liquor splashed all over his face until he finally found his mouth.

"Forget who?" asked Jerean. Panic began to set in on Jerean's face. She broke out in tears and experienced a slight shortness of breath. "Forget who? Who is he talking 'bout, Sis? Sis, who he gon get? We ain't done nothing to crazy Tweedy. Why he after us?" Her whimper increased with each question that couldn't be answered.

"Shut up, Jerean!" Sis sounded off angrily. "What's wrong with her?" she asked, looking at Etta. "What's wrong with you, girl? Why you crying? This ain't no time to be crying. This man out there trying to kill us. We need to be strong. I don't know 'bout you, but I ain't ready to see God. Etta, give me that knife," Sis insisted. She watched through the bottom of the window, "He must have seen the light come on."

Sis gave a hateful, but frightened look at Etta. "I told you not to cut that light on."

Tweedy recovered his posture and tilted his head up toward the porch ceiling. As thunder echoed across the sky, he slammed the whiskey bottle on the porch.

There came a moment of silence. Sis could no longer see Tweedy; he wasn't out there. It was as if he had disappeared. Inside, the house was quiet except for Jerean's sniffling.

Sis exploded with defined facial expression, "Stop crying, Jerean," her words were choppy, as tears began to run down her face, too. She could no longer camouflage her fear. Etta stretched out her arm until her hand lay upon Jerean's hand.

"Jerean," she whispered, "it's gon be okay. Daddy'll be home soon."

"Daddy ain't gon be home no time soon. If he ain't here by now, then he's working a double," Sis assumed.

With her face turned down, "It's all my fault," Etta cried.

11

Even though Sis was worried, she tried to comfort Etta.

"It's not your fault. It's nobody's fault. Tweedy doesn't have it all," Sis blurted.

Her eyes, red and burning from crying, Etta whimpered, "It's my fault. Sunday when Jerean saw Tweedy talking to me, he asked me why I looked so sad. He said, 'Why is the prettiest thing in the country so sad?' " Etta paused for several quick breaths and sniffles, then continued, "I took that as a chance to get a present, so I told him I wasn't getting anything for my birthday. I told him I wanted a cake. It was like he never heard me, because all he kept saying was that I was the prettiest gal in the country. Then when I saw Jerean coming, I got scared and pushed him away. I told him I didn't want nothing from a crazy old drunk. I only did it cause Deborah Potter was bragging 'bout what she was gon get for her birthday."

Sis went right to scolding her, "I told you Tweedy is crazy and now you don made that fool mad. Ain't no telling what he gon do."

"I'm sorry, Sis," she cried. "I just thought..."

Sis interrupted, "It makes no difference now, Etta. He wants to cut your tongue out. You pushed him and offended him, Etta. Ain't nobody ever done that to Tweedy and got away with it. Tweedy out to get you and anybody with you."

Sis's face was serious and she wished so much for her daddy to walk up on the porch at any moment.

Soon the rain let up and outside was quiet.

Wearied and scared, "Maybe he's gone," said Jerean.

"I hope," replied Sis.

Jerean leaned forward, hoping to see the porch deserted. She swiped her small thin hand across the window in an effort to wipe away the condensation. Quite suddenly, Tweedy's beady eyes were staring inside the window. Jerean screamed and fought her way back from the window. Shock penetrated her body as rigor mortis set in on her tongue. She pointed her finger towards the window. When her tongue finally loosened, she panted Tweedy's name. Emerging from a long silence, Tweedy began to stutter.

"You're the p-p-prettiest gal i-i-n town, Etta. I mean in the whhh-ole country." His words bounced off the ceiling and into their ears.

"You so p-p-pretty," he screamed. "You know w-w-what I'm gon do? I'm gon wr-write yo name in my book as the p-p-p-prettiest gal of them all. That's right, I-I-I'm gon do it and ain't no one gon stop me. You the prettiest gal in town," he professed, staggering in place, trying to reach the notepad in his back pants pocket. He scribbled in the notepad. "It's been done, a-and can't nooo-body change it. N-n-not even me," he said again and again.

Sis peeped at Jerean and Etta. "We got to get him off this porch or he liable to kill us. He done already killed Mr. Jennings, and he knows we saw him. Give me that knife now," Sis demanded. Etta had held it so tight that her fingers were swollen and sweaty.

Jerean began to panic, shaking her hands and flapping her legs in a frantic motion, "He gon kill us. He gon kill us." All of their faces reflected fright. That's when Sis demanded that something had to

13

be done. There was no telling when their father was coming home. It was either Tweedy or them.

"Etta, you and Jerean slide the door open and tiptoe on the porch. When he turns his back, jab him with the knife."

Sis held out the knife for someone to take.

"Nuh-uh!" they screamed, "you do it. You asked for the knife."

Tweedy began banging on the door again and kicking as well. The inside of the living room was in an earthquake of destruction: pictures, lamps, and mirrors were crashing to the floor with each of Tweedy's thunderous kicks. Then he stopped and turned around to face the street, turning the whiskey bottle up once again. Scoldingly, Sis gestured for Etta and Jerean to go onto the porch. Jerean didn't budge. Instead, Sis silently opened the door, "Etta, you got to go. You caused this problem, so you fix it."

She handed Etta the butcher knife. Etta could feel her hands shiver as she crawled onto the cold, wet porch. She trembled and turned to head back. "He gon catch me," she chattered nervously. The words were barely audible.

Once Etta was on the porch, she watched as Tweedy reached for the whiskey bottle. "Etta, my p-pretty. Today is the day," he said, turning slowly towards the front door.

"Do it now," Jerean demanded.

Etta hesitated; she was scared. Her body seemed to move in slow motion. She was frightened of the fact that she was about to kill a man. Tweedy bumped into the wooden post and was about to stagger upon her crouched body near the banister. Etta

14

saw him falling; there was no time to think, so she took off running. With one hard thrust, she lodged the knife through the trench coat and into his side, pushing her weight up against his body. She retrieved the knife, stepped back, and watched as his body suspended through the air for several long intense seconds, only to touch down in a filthy puddle of mud.

The lightning flashed and Etta's attention was caught by the reflection of the blade. Thick drops fell from its tip. She screamed and instantly threw the knife. She fled back into the house, feeling cold and disillusioned. Frantically, she began wiping her hands. Sis and Jerean remained quiet, standing at a distance, hesitant to approach her.

Sis spoke, "It's all right, Etta." Her voice was unsure. "It's over. Tweedy's dead."

A moment passed. They could hear Tweedy's heavy voice choking and coughing. Jerean leaped to the window.

"Hey y'all!!"

Tweedy had sat up in the mud and reached his hand underneath his heavy, feathered trench coat on the side where Etta had jabbed the knife. "I kn-now who did it," he screamed in agony. "I know you did it." Instinctively, Jerean stepped back from the window, "He gon get us now for sure!"

"I know you did it," he repeated, before pulling out a cake with white icing and red trim. The shape of the knife's blade was imprinted on the icing. The red trim had been smeared into the white. His eyes filled with anger as he contemplated throwing the cake into the front door.

"Naw, I know w-w-what I'm gon d-do. I'm taking y-y-yo name off my list. That's right y-you coming off d-dis list. Little nappy head girl, tr-tr-tried to give you a chance, and n-now you don't know how to act."

He rolled over in the mud onto his knees, then to his feet, staggering from one leg to the other. He dug into his back pocket and pulled out a dirty pad with a pencil stuck in the wire.

"You c-c-coming out my book if I got anything to do 'bout it." And he erased Etta's name as the prettiest gal in town. He stumbled into the street, pad in one hand and cake underneath his arm.

"Deborah Potter!" he screamed as he staggered down the street. "You the p-p-prettiest gal in town. And y-you know what I'm gon do? I'm gon write it in my book a-a-and once I write it, it can't ever be changed."

# PICKLED PIG FEET

# I.

My eyes probed the dull, gloomy gray walls that surrounded me, and I struggled hard not to think about the shame that would cause me to drown in my humiliation. Closing my eyes tightly, I wanted to trap myself inside my thoughts. My head dropped slightly; then slowly, gravity allowed my face to sink between my knees. An excruciating pain, a pain similar to an aching charley horse, throbbed repetitively in my lower abdomen. Automatically, my lower muscles tightened, causing the upper part of my body to bend in an effort to hold back the attacking pressure. Once the pain had subsided, I didn't bother to lift my head. Instead, I consciously followed my thoughts back to that morning.

Mom was bending down to get a skillet out of the lower cabinet. She slid the heavy iron pan over the largest of the burners on the stove as I stood in the kitchen doorway adjusting my red turtleneck for a more comfortable fit. She turned around and gave me a warm smile in greeting. We then commenced to converse, as was our normal routine.

"It's almost eleven o'clock and you just gettin' up?" she asked. "You gon sleep yo life away."

"I had to stay and take inventory at the store last night."

"Why?"

"Because that fat A…" I caught myself. "Mr. Scott picked me for the job as if he didn't see Jimmy's big butt sitting on the crate doing nothing. I know what's going on. Mr. Scott is trying to get up with

Jimmy's mother. That clown doesn't do a lick of work, so who gets the work? Moi."

I opened the refrigerator and leaned down to grab a soda. "But I ain't the one! I stayed there 'til almost two in the morning and still didn't finish."

"Uh huh," she said.

Ever since I was a kid, she had a habit of saying, 'uh huh', as if interested in the conversation when really she paid no attention. I figured she didn't want to be rude. She smiled, occasionally lifting her head to show her false attentiveness.

"Ma, you ain't listening to me."

"Honey, I'm sorry, but yo momma got a lotta cooking to do for church."

A large pot and a small frying pan were resting on the back burners; my eyes zoomed in closer to the stove. My mother was the best cook in the world—well, to me anyway. And the church congregation seemed to feel the same. There was nothing that she couldn't cook. She grew up in a small country town in North Carolina, learning from the elders the dos and don'ts of so many recipes. She removed a glass casserole dish from the oven and I inhaled deeply to tantalize my sense of smell.

"What are you cooking, Liz?" I called her by her first name as a way of teasing.

"That's candied yams," she replied and insisted, with a nod of the head, that she had no time for games today.

"Candied yams!!" I shouted with sudden jubilation. "What's in the pot?"

"Boilin' water for my taters. Move out the way now," she instructed, "so I can get to dis stove."

I slid to the side, but kept my eyes on the candied yams. "So what else are you cooking?"

With no hesitation, she began to call out the
foods on her preparation list.

"We gon have fluffy, mashed tatas and brown
gravy, some snaps, butta beans, black-eyed peas,
cone puddin', tater salad, macaroni 'n cheese, broccoli casserole, smothered cabbage, cone bread, hot butta
rolls, fried chicken, pineapple baked ham, roast beef,
meatloaf, Cajun fried catfish and trout, poke salad, a
small or large hen, I ain't decided, deep dish peach
cobbler...."

"Oh, Ma, you gon make it with peaches running
off the sides?" My tongue did an entire 360-degree
lick around my lips.

"Two-layer peanut butta'n chocolate cake,
sprinkled crust pound cake, and sweet potata pie. I'll
probbly fix a pecan pie, too. The pastor love pecan
pies."

"Is anybody else cooking?" I asked. I noticed on
the countertop that she had already prepared some of
the dishes. "Oh! They're just bringing an appetite."

Really, she wouldn't have cared if they didn't
bring a thing. She got pleasure out of cooking, whether it was a five-course meal for only two people or
a hundred. I guess that's why she cooked so many
church dinners. Since I enjoyed the food as much as
everyone else, I encouraged her to cook for any occasion (even for Wednesday night prayer meetings).

I took a long, sweeping step over to the counter
that held the prepared dishes. Gradually, I moved
from one dish to the other, taking deep inhalations
of each. That's when she said, "Well, if I have time,

I'll finish cooking them pickled pig feet." The words caught my attention immediately, as if she had blown a whistle. There was nothing I liked more nor food I would ever substitute for pickled pig feet. My anticipation was like that of an anxious child going to Disney World.

"Oh, Ma, for real, please cook'em. You know they're my favorite."

"If I have time."

"You got time to cook all that; of course you got time to cook pig feet. All you gotta do is boil'em. Oh come on, Ma, please. Don't make me beg."

Her expression was blank and silent.

"All right, I'll beg. Pleeeeeeeease!"

"Quinn," she said smiling, "maybe, if I have time."

If that was an attempt to shut me up, it worked. I licked my upper lip and then the bottom. The separation of my lips let off a subtle smack. I seated myself and then prepared to chow down.

"What's ready to eat now?" I asked, as the water gushed out of the faucet over a head of cabbage. There was no response. "Ma, you gon fix me something to eat?"

A large steel knife sliced through the cabbage head, semi-dissecting it. "You goin' to church tonight?" she asked.

"Tonight!? There's church tonight?"

"Yes, there's church tonight. Why you think I'm cooking all this food?"

"I thought it was for Sunday's church dinner."

"It's for tonight. So you comin' to church tonight?"

"No! Not tonight!" I cried out rudely.

There were two things you just didn't do in my mother's house: talk back or say you weren't going to church. If the circumstance wasn't life threatening or school-related, you were expected to be in church on Sundays.

"Tonight isn't a good night," I said, while my eyes stared at the floor.

She eased across the kitchen floor toward the pantry, her small eyes watching my face. Behind her smiling face, her eyes frowned.

"You not goin' to church? Then you don't eat," she simply replied, lugging a large bag of potatoes from the closet.

I rushed over to relieve her of the burden and paused a moment before untwisting the wire around the mouth of the sack.

"Come on, Ma. I have my reason for not going to church. Do you have a good reason not to feed your starving child?"

The more I found myself trying to escape this conversation, the more I was being pulled in. Usually, I could pour on the charm like thick gravy on mashed potatoes. However, she wasn't buying any of it today. Her head swung upward, eyes wide, and her body position and gestures made me feel that the next conversation was not one I wanted to get into.

"Get me dat basket uh cone on the back porch."

I returned with a bushel basket of corn.

"You ain't doin' nuthin; shuck that cone for me," she commanded. She hurriedly tossed the cabbage into the frying pan that had been warming up

22

with bacon grease. She sprinkled pepper and a little salt for taste.

"Hand me some uh dem taters," she ordered. "You wanna eat," she repeated, "then come to church tonight."

"Ma, ain't nothing but fools going to church tonight," I blurted without taking a second to think about what I was saying. I hid my face (because I knew she was offended), gritted my teeth, and pulled hard to remove the husk. She took everything personally. She had washed and peeled several po-tatoes before turning and walking to the center of the kitchen. I remained motionless, waiting for a backhand to my jaw at any moment. Sometimes the anticipation of a backhand flinched the face so tight that it hurt worse than the impact itself. She stood in the floor pondering as if she had forgotten some-thing.

Maybe she didn't hear me, I thought.

"Oh," she said softly. As she approached the counter, it was obvious that the beans had slipped her mind. In the other available sink, she placed the butter beans, black-eyed peas, and string beans into separate piles and drenched them using the water sprinkler. I twisted my head away from her with a sense of relief. When I turned back she was standing right beside me.

I jerked back and cautiously sat up in the chair.

"So, I'm a fool," she frowned.

"Huh?"

My eyes looked into hers with an apologetic smile. In an attempt to explain, I elected to choose my words carefully.

"Mom," I said calmly, hoping to make her aware of tonight's special occasion, "it's New Year's Eve. What I meant to say is who goes to church on New Year's Eve?"

"I do, the fool!" she chided loudly in a sassy tone. She had no intention of letting this conversation dwindle. "I been goin' to church on New Year's for mor'n twenty years."

"You have," I giggled before sipping the cola, and then ripping the corn husk some more.

"Boy, don't play wid me. Hand me that," she insisted, pointing to the sugar jar on the counter behind me.

With a handful of sugar in one hand and a wooden spoon in the other, she slowly allowed the sugar to filter between her fingers falling over the candied yams and the smothered cabbage. She stirred the cabbage leisurely, then added water, glancing over towards me again.

"There is church Sunday, right? So, I'll come Sunday." I grinned a victory grin—only later to shed it like cornhusks when she laid eyes upon my face.

"You missed church two Sundays straight, school-related, you say." She sounded very doubtful. I left the comment alone. Some things I had learned to just leave alone. She mumbled, "I have to fix some deviled eggs."

Oh, how I hated deviled eggs. I was directed by a pointed index finger. "Ma'am?" I asked.

"Get me that saucepan from the bottom cabinet."

At once I set aside the basket of cornhusks, and retrieved the saucepan. She was grabbing a casserole dish from the cabinet while I placed the saucepan on the stove. Before I could sit down and begin husking again, she ordered, "Get me that broccoli and a carton of eggs from the refrigerator. Get a block uh cheese while you at it."

I stopped, "Ma, is there anything else I can get while I'm up?"

"Pastor been askin' 'bout you."

I didn't reply.

"Quinn, you need to come to church. Let me ask you som'n. What do you like to do more than anything?"

"Dance," I replied.

"OK, when you don't eat, don't yo body get tired?"

"You won't feed me now and I'm tired," I said jokingly. "Yes, ma'am, I will get tired. And I know your next question befo you ask. Yes, I will not be able to dance."

"Because yo body ain't gettin' the nutrition it needs to stay healthy. Quinn, the same thing applies to yo spirituality. Son, you gotta feed yo spirit so ya can stay spiritually healthy."

"Ma, me missing a couple of Sundays isn't gon hurt me spiritually."

"OK, then missin' this meal shouldn't hurt you either."

I laughed, "You got jokes this morning."

"All right, Quinn." She paused and her eyes lit up. I knew she was up to something.

"What?"

"Caroline is gon be there."

"Oh, she is?" I tried to reply without showing any expressions of excitement.

Caroline is a brown-skinned girl with a perfectly round face sprinkled with freckles, and the most beautiful pair of amber eyes I had ever seen. She says she takes after her father. Why is it that mothers know all the right things to say to get you to attend church, even if it's for the wrong reasons? Her theory was that I might be there for one reason, but the Lord had another. Any other time, without the slightest hesitation, I would have chased the opportunity as a dog would a tractor-trailer but not tonight.

I whined softly, "Ma, I can't go to church tonight. The liveliest party of the year is tonight and the organization giving the dance is having a dance-off worth a thousand dollars. I'm so broke. When I dig in my pockets I can't even find lint. I got to win that money."

I said it with authority so she could have an idea of how important this was to me. I paused for a response. Her small vanilla hand unwrapped several sticks of butter and dropped them into a bowl. I watched as she meticulously churned the ingredients of milk, eggs, butter, flour, and nutmeg. I stood and placed the bushel basket of corn in the corner until she was ready for it.

"While you up, Mister Man, get me those two crock pots out the bottom cabinet."

"Which side?"

"The right side," she pointed. "So your great reason for not going to church is cuz you wanna go to a dance?" She exaggerated the words.

"Wouldn't you say a thousand dollars is a great reason?"

"Well, Quinn, the way I see it...."

Oh boy, here it comes. Whenever she said, "Well, Quinn," I knew it never favored me. I sat both crock pots on the counter and returned to my seat. I proceeded to fold my arms like a stubborn adolescent waiting for the inevitable.

"If God wants you ta have all dat money, He'll give it to ya. And if He don't, then it don't make a difference how much you feel for it, you'll never reach it."

Meanwhile I engaged in a puzzling thought. "How could God possibly not want me to have something? God's got bigger things to worry about. More important, why is the Bible so confusing?"

"Mom," my thought was bitter, but wisely hidden, "why do you always explain things using the Bible?" Sometimes deep within me, the topic of God or anything relating to God irritated my stomach some kind of terrible.

She said softly, "If God wants you to have it, He'll give it to ya. Trust Him."

My face mocked her scornfully. I added, "Ma, a lot of my friends are going to be there."

"The Bible says, 'When the blind lead the blind the two will fall into the ditch.' "

Now what did that have to do with me? I wasn't going with anyone blind, I thought.

"Does God not want me to have friends?" I asked, as my temperature began to rise.

"Sure God wants you ta have friends. There's plenty friends in the church."

"Naw, Ma, I want to see my friends and hopefully make some new friends."

"You can meet some new friends in the church."

"I don't think they want the type of friendship I'm offering—if you know what I mean." I winked. My temperature was now back to normal.

Suddenly she replied, "You got enough uh dem con-cu-bines callin' now." I gasped.

"Conkabines, what are conkabines?"

She turned, shaking a box of elbow macaroni towards me, "A hot-in-the-tail woman."

"Oh!" I smiled. "We call them freaks and hos."

"Watch yo mouth, boy."

"Well...."

"Well, whatever they are. You need a good Christian gal who don't reveal everything in a pair of body huggin' Dazey Dukes shorts. She leave something to the 'magination. She respects herself. Caroline is a good girl."

I couldn't stop laughing, "And what do you know about Dazey Dukes?"

"I know more'n you think I know."

I've already got too many bad girls trying to be good, I thought. Caroline was just too nice of a girl for me to take advantage of. I made her off limits.

"Ma, I can't go to church. I need money."

"Son, you need Jesus, and you can get Him for free."

"Depends on what church you go to," I muttered. I definitely didn't want to get into that conversation. "Mom, come on. I need to win this money."

She didn't say a word as she turned her back to me and went to take the cabbage off the burner.

"Quinn, get them chicken parts out the 'frigerator. I gotta get some mo containers."

"Are they in the freezer?" I asked before she

slipped out the kitchen and into the adjacent room, which was used for storing miscellaneous kitchen and laundry room items.

Her voice traveled from the back room, "No, in the bottom of the 'frigerator; they already thawed out. Just wash'em off."

I headed to the sink with the bag. "Wash yo hands befo you touch 'at chicken."

"Yes, ma'am."

Luckily, I heard the water boiling over on the burner before I saw it. My mother rushed in screaming, "Quinn, turn dat eye down."

She scared me into panic. Immediately I grabbed the pan with my bare hand to pull it off the burner, splashing scorching water on my hand. I was in agony. My mother had already turned the cold water on high for me to soak.

"Put yo hand under heah."

The chilling water began to overpower the burning sensation. It would be virtually impossible now for me to do a split into a spinning headstand, one of my patent moves.

"Don't you know yo own mouth can condemn you?" she asked, reducing the heat of the burner.

My entire concentration was devoted to blocking out the pain and thinking of a way I could still use the hand. I could hear my mother speaking in the background.

"Ma, what did you say?" I asked.

"I was just sayin' God don't like ugliness."

She gathered the peeled potatoes to put into the hot water.

"Who's ugly?"

With one hand, she took the container of bacon grease and caressed the burn, hoping to guard against any future scars.

"Get the gauze wraps out the first aid kit. I'll wrap your hand in a few."

She was experienced in taking care of people, so I did exactly as she ordered.

She rinsed off the chicken parts, and I watched quietly as she pulled the flour from the top cabinet. She poured two scoops along with some cornmeal and seasoning into a big, brown paper bag. I looked on in silence, unwilling to disturb her. She dropped a couple pieces of chicken into the bag and shook the bag vigorously. She then placed the chicken into the hot oil in the frying pan.

Finally, I broke the silence.

"How long you gon be in church tonight?" I asked in desperation, thinking maybe I could go early and make an appearance.

"From ten o'clock to long after midnight. And don't be puttin' God second in nuthin."

It was like she could read my mind.

"After midnight!" I shrieked. "No way. What is going on in church 'til after midnight? That's just when the party begins," I said, while gazing down at my greasy hand.

"Praisin' the Lord for gettin' us through anotha year. If you kin praise the devil every day of the week, you kin surely praise the Lord tonight. Start the year off right, Quinn."

"I plan on it by winning that money."

Her light complexion was turning red, annoyed at my stubborn behavior.

"Ma, I know you're familiar with the old saying, 'Whatever you're doing when the clock strikes
twelve on New Year's is what you're likely to be doing the entire year.' I want to be winning money. That
way I know I will have money all year round."

I sat back down, watching the grease popping
on each side of the pan until she covered it with a lid.

"Quinn, am I talkin' to myself? No matter how
much you wanna win that money, if it ain't God's
will, then it won't happen."

Attitude and force accentuated her words.
Words once spoken softly were now sharp and loud.
The way the conversation was evolving, it was obvi-
ous that we were headed for a collision. Of course,
I was too stubborn to listen. Finally, she broke away
from cooking to wrap my hand and wrist.

Aw, Ma is old, and what would she know anyway? I thought. "Ma, tonight I have to go win that
money," I said lastly before standing and slipping a
kiss on her pale cheeks. "Will you still cook me those
pig feet?"

"Come to church...."

I cut her words short. "Pray for me," I said, before going out the door.

"I always do, son."

## II.

That evening I broke through the back door
with urgency. My bladder was about to burst. I had
been in a crowded mall practically all day searching for a cheap outfit to wear to the dance. I ran
past Teddy, his upper body hunched over the stove.

I threw my bags on the bed and headed straight for the bathroom to relieve the fluid that had built since three o'clock that afternoon. My hand throbbed occasionally, and I was pretty sure I wasn't going to be able to use it for the dance. I was so thankful for Mike, my best friend since childhood, for lending me fifty bucks to buy an outfit.

These are the nineties and what could fifty bucks buy—especially at the mall? I thought as I drained six hours of pressure off my bladder in less than thirty seconds. However, I was always told that beggars shouldn't be choosy.

Once finished, I washed my hands and splashed some cold water on my face. I headed back into the kitchen in search of one thing—food. I was so hungry it felt like my stomach was scratching my spine. I stopped just inside the kitchen doorway. Teddy was standing now. He grabbed a bottle of Mad Dog 20/20 off the top of the refrigerator. He twisted the top in one smooth motion then took a long, continuous drink.

Teddy was my stepfather. His real name was Lewis, but everyone called him Teddy since his middle name was Theodore. Teddy came along after my father moved my mother and me to Virginia, and when he moved again he forgot to take us with him. Even though Teddy drank, I still had much respect for him. These days you see a lot of men making babies and abandoning the responsibilities to take care of them. So, it's not often that a man takes over a ready-made family. In addition to Teddy's occasional drinking, he had one other problem. He loved to mouth off at people. Honestly, he got more whippings than a worrisome two-year old. For plumbers, it's customary to come home with a few bumps and bruises; however, Teddy came home with more than a few black eyes. To each wound he credited not seeing a pipe or a sink when rising off the floor. There was a greater possibility that he didn't see the fist that was connecting to his face.

I stood in the doorway, watching with an awful taste in my mouth as he gulped every drop. Just watching him drink that poison brought a sickening feeling to my stomach. I can't say it was the alcohol that stunted his growth, but it definitely ruined his skin. His face was composed of several overlapping complexions. He turned towards me with blood-shot eyes and cracked lips.

"You want something to eat?" he asked, while twisting the cap back on the empty wine bottle.

I was so hungry, but I would starve before I ate anything Teddy cooked. He claimed, "I, Lewis T. Snead, can cook anything." He proved that when he barbecued a mouse. Ever since that day, no one ate Teddy's food except his friends. They're either insane or just too drunk to even care what it tastes like or even what it is.

I opened the refrigerator and scanned each rack for a covered plate. When I saw nothing, I slammed it, and maneuvered my way around Teddy to open the oven. It was empty.

Teddy staggered in place trying to hold his balance, "What, you want me to bake you something?"

"Do I want you to bake?" I said hatefully.

"Baking is my specialty; I won your momma over with my baking."

"What did you bake, bread?"

"You the one who can't cook, Chef Boy Ardee. "

As he rambled on, my eyes searched the stovetop. There was nothing except one covered pot.

"Teddy, did Ma leave me a plate of food?"

"She left a plate of food."

"Where is it?"

"I ate it."

"You ate it?"

"What do you suppose to do with food, Jacques Cousteau?" I hated when he called me that. I ain't no darn Jacques Cousteau, I thought.

"That was my plate of food," I declared to him, knowing, too, that it wouldn't change anything. I had my mouth waiting on that food all day, and that clown ate it. Today was not my day.

I stared at the pot on the stove as my blood boiled with anger. I removed the lid; the water was murky. My head tilted forward to take a sniff.

"What is this?" I asked. I looked about the kitchen to ask Teddy, but he had suddenly disappeared. "Good, I hope you go somewhere and lie down, sober up."

There in the dish rack was the wooden spoon Ma used this morning. I grabbed it and scoured through the dirty creek-like water. Floating to the surface was a combination of pig feet and pig ears, and the scent of pickle juice burned my nostrils.

"All right, Ma!!" I screamed. "Thank you!"

She had cooked my favorite—pickled pig feet.

"Well, my stomach will stop growling once it sees you," I mumbled.

I knew she couldn't stay upset with me. I began

singing as I prepared to eat. I searched the cabinet for the largest bowl I could find. With the wooden spoon, I pole-vaulted the pig feet and pig ears over into my bowl, then dripped a few dashes of vinegar and hot sauce, and a sprinkle of salt and pepper over them for extra flavor.

I sat down at the table, hovering over the bowl like a barbarian. Some of the pig ears and pig feet had a chewy and strange taste. I elected to disregard their taste by pouring additional vinegar and hot sauce over them.

This definitely isn't Ma's best. Cooking all day must have worn her out, I concluded. It took only twenty minutes to finish off four pig feet and three pig ears.

I pulled away from the table and tossed the bowl into the sink. The juice from the pig feet left a residue stickier than glue on my fingers, but that was nothing a little tongue action couldn't take care of. I licked them clean and then rinsed my hands before heading to my bedroom. Teddy was curled up on the sofa, resembling a baby with a pacifier (new bottle of wine) on the floor near his head.

I checked my watch; I was running late.

I had to take a shower, get dressed, and do my hair in less than thirty minutes. I itemized the time that would be needed for each.

"Five minutes for a shower, five minutes to get dressed, and twenty minutes for my hair. Yea, that's enough time," I said, dumping the new, fresh gear onto the bed. I dashed from the bedroom into the bathroom to run the shower. I peeled out of my clothes just as the phone rang.

"Teddy, get the phone," I screamed from the bathroom. "Teddy, get the phone!"

After four rings the answering machine picked up and Mike's voice screamed from the speaker.

"Mulatto, pick up. Mulatto, pick up."

Everyone called me Mulatto due to the fact that my mother was white and my father was black. I had always been told that if you have at least 10 percent of black blood in you, then you're considered to be black. To me, who cared about all this white, black issue—I was human. I kinda liked being called Mulatto because it didn't categorize me with any group.

I reached for a towel, and quickly swung it around my waist. Mike continued to yell.

"I know you're there; I just dropped you off not too long ago. Pick up, fool."

As soon as I stepped out of the bathroom, the cool air forced the hairs to stand up on my skin. Just as he was about to hang up, I reached for the receiver. "What's up?"

"Man, what took you so long?"

"I was in the bathroom taking a shower. Now what's so important?"

"Be ready man when I come through."

"I'll be ready."

"Mulatto, I know you. It takes you twenty-five minutes to do your hair. Man, you're worse than a woman."

"Well, women and I have something in common."

"What?"

"Beauty takes time to perfect; it's like fine wine."

"Well, I tell you what. If your beauty hasn't reached you in thirty minutes, then you'll have all night to wait on it. I'm hitting the horn only twice."

"What's up with Ice, Fella, and Joe?"

"They're going to meet us at the party."

"All right kid, I'm out. See you in thirty. Peace."

"Out."

## III.

By the time I showered and got dressed, Teddy was sitting on my bed with a bottle of Black Suede cologne in his hand.

"Why do you have that in your hand?" I asked, positioning myself in front of the full-length mirror, browsing over my attire. I gazed at my reflection. Was I smooth, or what? Yes, this would be my night.

"You think you Don Juan of the Ghetto?"

I laughed, "Man, you crazy."

Teddy lay back on the bed. His eyes were focused on the ceiling, "How'd my Black Suede get so low?"

"I know you don't think I've been wearing that!? I haven't gotten that desperate yet."

"Your momma sure ain't wearing it."

I focused on my outfit, wiping the lint off, adjusting the gig line, and making sure it fit perfectly. A few of the buttons on my pants were loose. Without my mother here to sew them, I just had to hope they didn't come off.

One of the strings from a very loose button was hanging. As I was wrapping it underneath the button, Teddy sat up on the bed.

"You think you look flawless, huh?"

I fanned my hands over my outfit. "I am flaw-less."

"Boy, you twenty-four cents away from a quarter. How you flawless?"

"Because it ain't in the money."

"It ain't in the pockets either."

"Since you mentioned it, Teddy, I need ten dollars for the dance tonight."

"Sounds like a personal problem to me. Things that personal, I try not to get involved."

"Come on, Teddy, I'll pay it back."

"See, that's what's wrong with you and them other stupids you hang with. Ain't never got no money and expect some woman to call you. Women don't want no broke man."

He clicked his fingers together. "What's that woman's name?"

"What woman?"

Again, he clicked his fingers, "You know, the one who sings that song 'No Romance Without Finance.' "

"Man, you know how old that song is?"

"It ain't that old."

"Old enough."

"Well, it still applies to you," he chuckled loudly and repeated, "No romance without finance. If you don't have any money, why you getting dressed?"

"So I can win a thousand dollars, but I need ten dollars to get in."

Teddy got off the bed and stood up.

"If you had some game like me," he expressed with a slap on his chest, "you would've had a lady buy you a ticket, mail it to you, and pick you up to take you to the dance."

I stood aside, watching through the mirror as Teddy exited the bedroom and re-entered with a wine bottle. I heard the cracking of the top as he un-screwed it. He took a quick chug and said, "I can get you some Black Suede without you stealing all of mine."

I moved him aside. "Teddy, Black Suede is older than Methuselah. Why would I want to wear that?" I leaned forward to reach the pomade container on the dresser, flipped off the top and rubbed several large dollops into my hair.

"That's why Methuselah lived so long; he wore Black Suede. Why you putting that poison in yo hair? It ain't gon do nothing but ruin yo hair. Instead of calling you Rico Suave, they'll be callin' you Snappy Nappy from the No Comb Tribe. I used to have real natural hair." He slid his hand over what used to be there.

"Yeah, right."

"I did until your mother put that perm in my head—messed my hair up," he said as he lay back on the bed. "My hair won't even grow now."

"The pomade is to lay it down."

Teddy gave me a stupid look. He paused and then scrutinized my pants.

"Them my bell-bottoms you wearing?"

"These are not yours," I said in defense. "I just bought these pants." I smiled and squinted my eyes at him. "These are denim boot-legged pants."

They had thick white stripes running down the sides. I was wearing a long-sleeved, black mock turtleneck with a white stripe down the center that really set the outfit off.

"Just a wannabe bell-bottom. I suggest you get a pair of mine, but give'em back."

"Don't flatter yourself, because I'll never be caught in yours."

He staggered into the kitchen, "I knew my pants were coming back in style. That's why I saved six boxes of'em. All I need is for the fly collars to come back in style. What do y'all youngin's say, 'I'll be off the hook'?"

I could hear him yelling from the kitchen, "Go in the closet and put on my platform shoes, then you'll have game."

When Mike bumped the horn, I glanced at my watch. I had over five minutes to spare. Teddy stood in the center of the kitchen floor, smiling broadly with ten dollars in his hand.

"Don't spend it all in one place," he said.

When I came out the back door, Mike had already turned the car around in the driveway with the engine idling. I closed the screen door, not realizing my pants had gotten stuck on a protruding hook used to hang Christmas lights. The pants ripped and every button popped off. It was like something out of a sitcom.

"Can you believe this?" I screamed. "What else can happen to me tonight?" Fifty dollars had gone down the drain that fast. I didn't have anything else to wear.

Mike got out of the car and yelled, "What's the holdup?"

"My pants just ripped," I told him as he approached.

"We don't have much time, so hurry up and go change."

I opened the door and we went back into the house. Teddy was standing between the living room and kitchen entrance.

"What, the woman just as broke as you? And who did you bring with you but another member of the 'Five Heartbeats'."

"Show some compassion, will you? My pants just got caught on the door."

"Hey, Mr. Snead."

Tonight was not going to be shattered by a pair of pants; I had to find something to wear, I thought.

"Come on back, Mike."

"Come on back, Mike," Teddy echoed.

All he needed was one person as an audience to perform for. While he gathered material, I searched through the dresser drawers for a pair of pants. I found a pair with polka dots. "I can't wear these." I picked up another pair that was worse than the first and immediately slammed them down.

Teddy laughed, "It's a mountain of dirty clothes in the corner. I'm sure you can find something, but stay away from them dirty draws, boy. Looks like they got drag strips in'em."

"Word! Not drag strips, Mr. Snead," Mike laughed.

Teddy took another swig. "Go on and wear something dirty, and if anybody smells something, blame it on the person next to you."

"I don't care if he finds something dirty or clean, but we got to roll," Mike said.

"Mike, can't you see I'm going through a crisis here?" My head was about to explode. "Come on, man, help me find something."

"This ain't my room," he shook his head and moved back into the kitchen.

Teddy watched, "I don't blame you, son. It might rub off on you."

They both were really upsetting me; then it came to me.

"Teddy, where are those pants of yours?"

"Not my bell-bottoms—not the ones you wouldn't be caught dead in."

"All right, Teddy. You win. I need'em."

"Come on, Mulatto; we gotta roll."

"Teddy, are you going to let me wear them?"

"Go 'head, but don't mess'em up. Anything over twenty years old is supposed to be an antique, collectors item, or something like that."

"What difference does it make? You plan on paying taxes on them?"

I searched through the box and found a pair. Not bad, I thought, except for that huge silver buckle and the extremely wide-legged bottoms. They extended completely over my boots. I had to be careful not to trip. Mike came around the corner and burst into hysterics when he saw me in the tight, black polyester bell-bottoms.

"Kid, you look like a member of the Commodores."

Teddy walked into the room and said, "Least you don't have that big head like Lionel Ritchie."

IV.

We arrived outside the hotel around 11:30 p.m. There was an influx of people entering the hotel lobby. It was customary for the guys to meet before going into a dance. And this night would be no exception. I spotted them in the corner by the ballroom doors, checking out ladies as they entered and exited. A large sign near a beautiful fountain read, "Count Down to the New Year" and "Win 1000 Dollars." My eyes lit up with dollar signs.

"Are you ready to win that loot?" Ice asked, as his head nodded me towards a beautiful red-bone that was coming through the hotel's door.

"Yeah! I'm ready to win a whole lot of things," I suggested in a presumptuous manner. "Ice, I got to win that money."

"You mean we got to win that money."

"Whatever."

Fella and Joe were preoccupied with two women who were very well known to the entire group.

I got Ice's attention, "Yo, are Fella and Joe kicking it with them?"

"Now, you know they ain't even trying to get up with them chicken-heads." Ice gave a quick wave for Joe and Fella to come over.

"Man, what are y'all doing talking to those ugly chicken-heads?" I asked.

Fella tried to talk his way out of it. "They ain't ugly; they just unattractive."

"I don't know, man. Times are hard. Lately, I can't turn nothing down but my shirt collar," was Joe's pathetic reply.

Fella gazed at my hair and broke into a laugh, which soon turned into hysteria when he saw my pants up close.

"Mulatto, I have two questions for you. First, what is that in your hair? Second, what are you wearing?"

"You got more grease in your head than the majority of these women in here," mocked Mike.

"Mulatto, I need some grease for my hands because I'm a little ashy," Joe teased.

They all hackled like a pack of hyenas. "All right. Y'all can laugh, but when I win that money, don't even look my way."

As I peeled away from the jackals, Summer was coming in from the cold. She could bring sunshine to anybody's rainy day. I strolled over to a vase of beautiful flowers that were kind of withering from the cold. I snuck up behind her; the guys were watching. I slipped the flowers over her shoulder.

"I saw these flowers about to die, and I figured with the cold air blowing on them, just a glimpse of Summer would revive their petals."

"Save the drama," she blurted. She caught me off guard.

"Look at ya, hair all greased up, wearing your daddy's pants." I looked around confused, because I hadn't told anyone. She continued, "Always shooting lines."

"Hey, next time tell your boy not to run a similar line on me," her friend said, then rolled her eyes in my direction.

Summer's eyes were spiteful, "What, no new lines to tell the ladies?"

After gathering my thoughts, I managed to gather my pride and my face. "Well, let me be the first to apologize for my friend, because what are lines but words carelessly tossed about, controlled by a tongue that is crafty? And I sympathize with you, for those useless words have no sincerity. They undermine the capacity of your mind, turning your heart bitter." I moved closer to her, "Now, your words are like a torrential storm seeking destruction."

My words were spoken gently in a low tone. Her eyes no longer vented anger, and her words were no longer parched with dryness. Instead, a smile bloomed upon her face, as a flower would in her season.

"You see," I said, "that was all I wanted."

With poise, I handed her the flowers and walked away, leaving her shield crumbled at her feet.

V.

I glanced around the crowded ballroom. Summer was right in front, watching me as I watched her. I didn't need that added pressure. My fingers began to tremble, but not because I was nervous. I admit there was some fidgety energy, but nothing that should have made me tremble or break out in a cold sweat. My love of dancing had always allowed me to successfully overcome the butterflies. I examined the other dancers waiting anxiously to get on the dance floor. One thousand dollars brought the best hip-hop dancers from my area and the surrounding areas.

Dancers starved for the opportunity to win some big money. In all, there were about twenty dancers. There were only two I had devoted my attention to: Kyle Richards and Sassy Tee. Kyle Richards was from out of town, well-known for his relentlessness and funky dance moves. Sassy Tee was the best female dancer in the area; she had moves that were electrifying. No one thought I had a chance to win since I was considered the new kid on the block; and with my injured hand, I would be forced to come up with some new moves. Still, I wasn't too worried, since I had practiced over fifty dance moves.

The Disc Jockey turned down the music and screamed into the mic, "Let me hear you say Heyyy, Hey."

The crowd repeated, "Heyyy, Hey."

"Let me hear you say HOoo, ho."

"HOoo, ho!"

"When I say Hip, you say Hop,.........HIP."

"Hop!" cried the crowd.

"Now somebody, anybody, everybody SCREAM!"

"AHHHHHHHHHH!" in unison.

The energy in the room was pure off the hook (electric).

"All right, all right. My name is DJ T-Cal and tonight's dance competition is sponsored by the Limelight Social Club. Dancers were pre-qualified to participate in this New Year's Eve dance competition." The crowd gave another roar.

"All right, all right, calm down so I can read the rules. Dancers are to perform old school and new school dances. There will be thirty-two minutes of continuous dance, forty-five seconds to do each move and three seconds to transition into another move.

You should have a continuous variation. This equates to a minimum of forty dances if a dancer utilizes the entire forty-five seconds on a dance move. No dance can be performed by the same dancer twice, and dancers cannot be physically supported by anyone, nor can they leave the dance floor at anytime. If so, they risk being disqualified. Dancers are to dance from the time I say start to the time I say Happy New Year!" The crowd screamed even louder.

"Now various individuals are placed around the perimeter of the dance floor to make sure all dancers stay within the rules. There will be three judges: a choreographer for several major music videos, a representative from the Limelight Social Club." DJ's voice was already becoming hoarse as he screamed, "And YOU, the crowd. Now dancers will be judged on their creativity, style, energy, and endurance. I hope you all have a lot of dances in your arsenal because you're going to need them."

DJ T-Cal looked around the room, "Dancers, ARE-YOU-READY?" It was so loud it felt as if the roof was about to blow.

The crowd was completely out of control and so was DJ T-Cal. He raved on, "Are you ready?"

"Yeeeaaahhh!"

With the noise level at its pinnacle, so was my adrenaline. If I didn't hurry up and release some of this energy I was going to explode. I kept hearing my stomach growl, but I wasn't hungry. Ignore the feeling and blame it on my excitement to get started, I thought. All the guys gathered around me for last-minute encouragement. I was ready; I couldn't be any more ready.

Fella leaned over and looked me in the face. "Man, your eyes don't look right," he said, taking his fingers and pulling down the bottom lid. "Are you okay?"

"I don't know," I gasped.

"What do you mean you don't know?" he asked with concern.

He was beginning to irritate me. I inhaled deeply and said, "Look, Doogie Howser, I don't know, so leave my eyes alone."

Mike screamed over top of the DJ's voice, "All right, Mulatto. Break'em off."

DJ T-Cal began his countdown, "Ten, nine, eight..."

The crowd chanted along, "Seven, six, five..." I adjusted the contestant number over my chest. I couldn't believe it; I was actually nervous. The butterflies, which I hadn't felt in years, were flying everywhere in my stomach. They must be kamikaze butterflies, I thought.

Two large tanks lying on the floor sprayed out a misty fog that completely hid the dance floor. You could feel the vibration the speakers were giving off.

A voice from a record said, "Pump, Pump, Pump, Pump it up!"

"Let the dance-off begin!!" yelled the DJ, then followed by screaming, "old school!" His intro was Salt and Pepper's, "My mic sounds nice, check one, my mic sounds nice, check two, are you ready?" DJ T-Cal came back with a hard baseline by Special Ed, "I Got It Made...Dummp, domb'dah, domb'dah ..............Dummp, domb'dah, domb'dah."

He made his transitions from record to record quickly. Scratching in with, "What time is it? Put your Gucci watch on, synchronize the time, and let's rock.....dot,... dot.da.da.dot."

As everyone else did, I started out with a couple of basic moves to get a feel for what the judges were looking for. I didn't want to dance too fast or use up my creativity. That notified the judges you were out of ideas. DJ T-Cal mixed in an old classic Eric B & Rakim joint, "It's been a long time, I shouldn't have left you...." He kept the pace of the music with RUN-DMC's, "My Adidas, walk through column doors, and roam all over coliseum floors...." I heard the DJ scratch hard on the turntables before screaming through the mic, "You know what, Loddy-Doddy, we like to party, we don't cause trouble, we don't bother nobody, we're...." He came in hard with Wu Tang Clan, "I grew up on the crime side, the New York Times side, staying alive was no jive." Then Snoop Dogg and Dr. Dre's voices filtered through the speakers, "With so much drama in the L-B-C it's kinda hard bein' Snoop D-O-double-G, but I...." The rhythm of the record began to slow, then abruptly it sped up to its normal playing speed. Outkast faded in...me and youuuu, yo momma and yo cusin' toooo, rollin' down the strip on vogues comin' up slamin'...." He came back with, "Milk is chillin', Giz, is chillin' what mo can I say top billin', that's right I get it, I got it good, if you understood, would you clap your hands, your hands you clap...."

An echo of clapping vibrated around the room. Rhythmically pumping their fists in the air, the crowd shouted, "Go head! Go head! Go head!" My muscles were warming up, flexibility increasing with every full range of motion.

I was doing the Roger Rabbit that easily transformed into the Smurf. I looked around and the crowd was feelin' me, and I was feelin' the music. After ten minutes into the dance-off, over half of the dancers had been eliminated. Kyle Richards gracefully cruised across the floor like a brand new Cadillac Eldorado for everyone to catch a glimpse. His footwork was fascinating. A wax couldn't put on a better shine. I marveled at his gracefulness. Sassy Tee performed her rendition of the Lil' Kim, a dance that heated up the synovial membranes around her joints, making Sassy Tee even more agile to maneuver some of her more difficult dances.

To pass the time, I broke into old school dances that my mother and grandmother used to do: Hammer, Buck, Shimmy shoowobby, Watoosy, Mashed Potato, Swim, the James Brown, Twist, Rock, Fly, the Jerk, and Surf.

I was sweating profusely. Continuous hip-hop dancing is not as easy as everyone assumes. It requires me to work every muscle in my body. I definitely needed great stamina to win.

Kyle glided over and spun Sassy Tee around. They commenced with the Hustle. I did my best hip hop imitation of John Travolta's "Saturday Night Fever." Before I knew it, we were the only three on the floor.

I cut my eyes over to Sassy Tee and Kyle. Darn they're good, I thought.

With only three of us left, I knew the judges would be even more scrutinizing. I wanted to save my best moves for last, since last impressions stay on the mind. I shifted from move to move: the MC Hammer, Snake, Kid-n-Play, Dookie Booty, Dodo Brown, Alf, Detroit Hustle, Shuffle, Face Off, the Prep, Raising the Roof, the Pepperseed, the Puffy, the Running Man, and Gettin' Jiggy. Sporadically, I would attempt a spin move, but I felt nauseated each time.

Unexpectedly, the DJ sounded another horn that screamed much like a fire engine, "wharrrrrmmm."

"REWIND!" the voice over the record screamed. "Daddadadadadadadadadad, it's time for the percolator. " A minute later the DJ mixed in a hot track by Sean Paul.

I was too tired to perform anything other than a simple, slow imitation of the whop, hoping to preserve some energy for later. I figured, however, that they had to be just as tired. I looked over to investigate. Kyle was moving slower than me, but Sassy Tee was working it out with the Pepperseed. At the moment, there was no way I could keep up with her, but I had a plan. I knew that the New Year's hour was upon us, and the DJ normally waits to play the fastest cuts towards the end of the competition. Then I would make my move.

Suddenly, there came a police siren from the speakers followed by a loud explosion. The DJ yelled, "New School!" His intro was Clipse, "Star Trek... when the last time you heard it like this, smoke somethin', drink smothin' get ripped. The record zigzagged over Lil' Wayne's...Go DJ...Cuz that's my DJ...go DJ."

He went on to remix Jay Z, 50 Cents, DMX, Fat Joe, JaRule, Jada Kiss ,Ying and Yang Twins, Twista,

Nas, Cam'ron, Mob Deep, Xizibit, Lil' Flip, 8 Ball and
MJG, Lil John and the Eastside Boyz, P. Diddy, Fabo-
lous, Red Man, Method Man, Jim Jones, Young Buck,
Obie-Trice, MJG, Ice Cube, Biggie, TuPac, Pharrell,
Timberland, Missy Elliot, Trick Daddy, Lloyd Banks,
Ghetto Boy, Scareface,T.I., Eminem, The Game and
many more hip-hop artists.

Less than fifteen minutes remained. I knew
Sassy Tee had given her best, but not Kyle. He had
rested and only demonstrated a simple Bank-Head-
Bounce, to Master P's "Bout It, Bout It," and was
waiting, as I, for the last minute.

The music DJ T-Cal played had taken me into a
zone. I started into some favorite old school dances:
the Reebok, the School Craft, The Food Stamp, the
Paddy Duke, the Cabbage Patch, the Coca-Cola, then
I graduated to more modern dances like the Down
Low, the Rock Away, the St. Louis Chicken, the One-
Two Step, the Muscle, the A-Town, the J-Wood Throt-
tle, and the Heal Toe.

I was slamming it, flashing from one move
to another. I got so hyped when the crowd started
shouting my name, "Go Mulatto! Go Mulatto!" If I
had the crowd on my side, it was only a matter of
time before I had the other two judges. Plus, I hadn't
even done my new patent move. I could sense that
Kyle and Sassy Tee were staring.

"Go Mulatto, go Mulatto," they urged and I did,
breaking into more funky moves, when all of a sudden
I felt something wet run down the inside of my leg.
It definitely caught my attention. What's going on? I
thought. Then another drop drizzled down my leg.
The crowd and I both wondered what I was doing.

"Ahhh," I murmured.

A piercing pain stabbed me in my side. Another sharp pain hit me under my ribs. I had no choice but to stop. The pain was so bad in my lower abdomen it forced me to hunch over. Funny grumbling sounds came from my stomach and then two more sharp pains. Immediately, I clinched my butt cheeks together, my face was full of embarrassment. I wanted to move, but I couldn't. Another stream had begun to fall. I squeezed even tighter to keep in whatever was trying to come out.

"Surely this couldn't be happening to me—not here," I moaned, knowing I had only a few seconds to create a move.

Fella's eyes tunneled in on me. "What are you doing?"

I tried telling him, "I can't move," but the music was too loud for him to hear me.

The DJ announced, "I think we might have another contestant eliminated if he can't perform a move in three seconds."

What move could I perform without a move occurring within me? I wondered uneasily as the guys demanded I do something.

I vaguely heard Mike say, "He's doing the Robot."

Yeah, I thought, the Robot.

With my buttocks tighter than ever, I mechanically moved each of my limbs. Dizziness began to come over me. I felt like throwing up.

Oh no! Here it comes again, as tugging cramps plunged into my stomach.

"Mulatto," waved Joe with his hands.

53

"You only have thirty seconds; you're too close, kid," remarked Fella.

I agreed with an assuring nod that I could make it. With difficulty, I slowly dragged my body from one direction to another. Unexpectedly, the pain diminished. It was as if it had never happened. I relaxed my buttocks and my abs.

"Thirty seconds left," I heeded. Half of the crowd rooted for Kyle, the other for Sassy Tee. I had lost momentum; obviously I had to do my patent move in order to win. I was cautious because I didn't know what was going on with my body. The countdown to the New Year began. "25, 24, 23, 22...."

I was going to let it all out. I began spinning and pop locking, swooping through the air. The crowd said, "Oooooooooh." I landed into my patent Nicholas Brothers' split. Abruptly, that's when it all split (and it rhymed with split), coming down both legs. My stomach had no contracting ability.

"19, 18, 17...," said the crowd. I looked around, tucked my butt in and bounced to my feet. It ran into my boots. I charged past the guys, bursting into the bathroom, then into the gray stall. The pain hit again and somehow I knew there was more to come.

"This darn belt," I grumbled, tugging at it. I couldn't get it undone. I squirmed and bounced, pulling harder; it was still coming; nothing else for me to do, but snatch them off. The mudslide came with full force. What embarrassment, I thought, as it was all over me. The New Year was approaching and then I recalled what I had said earlier to my mother, "Whatever you're doing when the clock strikes twelve is what you'll likely be doing the entire year."

## VI.

My tee-shirt was soaking wet, I rolled over in the bed and it felt like somebody had taken a sledgehammer to my intestines. I flung the shirt into the corner. My diarrhea didn't stop at the dance, but lasted all night. Just then the door to my bedroom opened. I can't remember ever being so happy to see my mother's face.

"Good morning."

In pain, "Good morning."

"How did it go last night?"

"It was a disaster."

"What happened?"

"Trust me, you don't want to know, nor do I want to relive it."

She forced me to tell her what happened in detail and after I finished she laughed so hard that tears streamed down her face.

"So you didn't win?"

"No, ma'am, I didn't. A dancer named Sassy Tee won."

"I'm not gon' rub this in, baby," she said snickering. "But it don't make a difference what you do, if God ain't in it, baby, it won't work."

My eyes filtered upward, "I'll be in church this Sunday." Then came a wave of cramps, locking my stomach up again.

She took the back of her hand and laid it on my forehead. "My baby is sick. Quinn, you're burning up. Have you taken anything?"

"No, ma'am."

"I'll get the Castor oil."

"No!" I screamed. "No way, I didn't like it when I was young and I can't stand it now."

"Boy, lie down."

Before she lifted herself off the bed I whined, "Ma, I don't want no pig feet anytime soon."

"Pig feet?" her expression was baffled.

"Don't take this the wrong way, but your pig feet ain't never tasted that bad."

She gave me a puzzled look. "Quinn, you didn't eat those pig feet, did you?"

"Yes, ma'am, I did."

She paused, "Teddy."

I sat up, "What about Teddy? Did Teddy cook'em?"

"Quinn," she said slowly, "them pig feet was raw, baby. He was supposed to cook'em."

"You telling me I ate raw pig feet?"

"You might get trichinosis. Get dressed so I can take you to the doctor." She rose off the bed and headed for the door.

"Wait a minute, what is Tri – cha – nosis? Ma, don't leave the room. What's Tic-ca – nosi. TEDDY!!!"

# MOE BROWN

# I.

Rudy Alexander sat on his small, wooden front porch watching the hot vapors rise off the street. He took a dirty, blue bandanna and fought tirelessly to wipe the sweat from his face and head of partially shaved salt-and-pepper hair. His large frame fit snugly into an old beat-up rocking chair that squeaked with every forward motion and his teeth clamped tightly down on an old corncob pipe. It was relaxing to him to watch the sequences of smoke rings he so carefully exhaled. In his solitude, he found refuge rocking leisurely as the sky turned from a clear blue to a dusty orange. He was interrupted when Moe Jackson sauntered into the front yard with wide eyes and a serious temper.

"Mr. Alexander," he said cautiously, swaying and digging both of his hands deep into his front overall pockets. "Will you make yo dauder marry me? I may look crazy, but I sure as hell ain't stupid. Sir, I been datin' yo dauder fo a long time now, and I know she been foolin' roun' with dat Harry Brown. I know! Every time I come ova heah, there Harry Brown is. My momma ain't raised no fools—not saying that you did, but I don had it up ta heah," Moe swiftly gestured a slice across his neck.

He figured that getting Rudy to force her would end all the competition between Harry Brown and himself. Rudy continued to puff on his pipe, fogging Moe's vision. Moe fanned the smoke out of his face and continued his plea.

"Sir, I know I ain't got no right to be comin' ova heah wid a lot of demands, but I love Juanita and I'll

damn sho take good care ov'er. You bess believe dat,"
he asserted with a stomp on the ground. "See, I just
got hired on at the sawmill and my daddy say, 'All
a man need is a good job an' a good woman.' I don't
have the bess education, but I got good common
sense. And ya wanna know what my common sense
telling me?" Rudy didn't answer. "It's telling me,
'Moe, enough is enough. Either she want you or she
want him'." Moe inhaled deeply through his nostrils
and released the air with a new sense of confidence.

Rudy scrutinized the tall, skinny, dark-skinned
boy standing boldly in front of him. Their eyes
caught for a moment and then glanced away. He released his grip around the pipe and grabbed a large
Mason jar half full of home-brewed apple brandy,
which was sitting on the tree stump table beside him.

Rudy was notorious in Clarksville as "Big Rudy
the Gun Shooter." Even though he never actually
shot anyone, he was known for always toting a .22
snub nose pistol. Rumor had it that he had killed
more men than cancer. Rudy couldn't boast that lie,
but he never argued against it either. Most rumors
were spread by local drinking buddies—friends
Rudy acquired every Friday through Sunday who
came from Clarksville and surrounding counties to
buy some of the best homemade wine around. They
had yet to find another wine that could satisfy them
like Rudy's. Rudy cut his eyes over towards Moe
and made a series of short, grotesque noises, before
spitting a wad of saliva over his left shoulder. Moe
stared warily, not knowing if he had offended Mr. Alexander with his sudden demands. Rudy hitched the
rocker forward; it let out a gentle squeak.

"Nita! Nita!" Rudy called in a nasal tenor voice. A thin, petite girl came to the doorway, pressed her face against the screen and let out a shallow gasp of exhaustion. "Yes, Daddy, you need another fill?" she asked, while slipping her tiny frame between the barely opened screen door.

She reached over to get the empty Mason jar from the old tree trunk.

"In a minute," Rudy replied, again hitching the rocker forward. This time staring directly into Moe's eyes, "Ya want dis' boy?" he asked suddenly.

Juanita stood quietly with a blank look about her.

"Well, ya want him? The boy say he wanna marry ya."

Rudy took his eyes off of Moe and placed his gaze on Juanita. "Cause I'm tired of'em both comin' roun' heah bristlin' at each other. Not at my house," he gnashed. He focused his eyes back on Moe and continued to rock slowly.

Before Juanita could respond, Moe fell to both knees with his hands in praying fashion, "Please, Juanita, I love ya. I'll love ya more'n dat Harry Brown ever will, and ya know it."

Juanita looked dumbfounded. Placing one hand on her chest, "Me?" she asked with false disbelief. "He wanna marry me, Daddy?"

"Dat's what the boy said."

She would be lying if she said she didn't like the fact that two men were fighting over her; she loved it. She loved her camaraderie with the two and more importantly, she loved the benefits of having them both. But no matter how much she loved it, she knew it wasn't pleasing to God, and her spirit was convict-

ing her. Now Rudy, too, was giving her an ultima-
tum. God is used to taking his time, but Rudy wasn't.
God and Juanita knew that Rudy was never one for
patience. He meant business. Plus, she figured Harry
would never ask to marry her. He would often say he
wasn't the marrying type.

While Moe pleaded for her hand, a wide smile
stretched from one side of Juanita's face to the other.

"Yes, Daddy, I'll take him."

"You will?" screamed Moe, quickly jumping up,
clicking his heels together.

It scared Rudy so badly he reached into his trousers and pulled out his .22. He waved the gun in the
air, stopping as his aim reached Moe. Moe restrained
his sudden jubilation.

"Boy, ya gotta carry dat foolishness somewhere
else befo I shoot ya. Don'tcha know I'll shoot ya?"

"Yessuh, that's what I heard."

It wasn't that Rudy disliked Moe; he hated all
the boys that courted Juanita. He grew up being treated that way by other fathers, so he figured he'd dare
not change tradition now. Juanita was his only daughter, so he was going to make sure no one hurt her.

Moe could feel his own throat quiver as Rudy
pointed the barrel of the pistol at the center of his
face.

Rudy spoke calmly, "Somethin' don't soun'
right. All of a sud'n you wanna marry Nita. Dat don't
soun' fishy to you?" Moe could feel the cold sweat
run down the front of his forehead. The pressure
from the sight of the gun confused Rudy's question.

"Yes, sir."

"I know it does."

"Now what I want to know..." he stopped temporarily and thought about the question himself. His eyebrows frowned inward and his eyes squinted. "Is my dauder pregnant, boy?" he yelled.

The question hit Moe's ears like fingernails being dragged across a chalkboard. Moe looked at Juanita for help.

His words stalled, "Aw, Aw, nawsuh, not that I know of. I mean not by me."

Rudy pushed the gun forward, "What?"

"Sir, I don't know! She a virgin, ain't she?"

"She bedda be!"

No one said anything for at least five minutes. Then Rudy lodged the gun back into his front pocket and took his seat in the squeaky rocker. He shoved the pipe back into his mouth and focused his attention on the newlywed couple up the street. The young girl was pregnant and her husband was yelling at her.

"One more thing," he said as he stared at the couple. "I don't believe in no shotgun wed'ns. I rather kill the man than have my dauder marry some no good Negro; save her an' the baby a lotta trouble down the road."

Moe stood in the yard, quiet and alert.

Juanita had to break the silence, "Daddy, you want me to get you another jar of brandy?"

"Naw, I'll get it. I gotta make another batch anyway befo the stragglers come by on their way to the juke joint."

Rudy lifted himself out of the rocker and dragged himself over to the door. A wound from an old job accident prevented him from bending his right knee, so he dragged it instead. Juanita pulled the front door open for him to pass. Rudy gave Moe a long and intense glare, then kissed Juanita on the cheek. "If you need anything, I'll be in here."

## II.

When Moe thought the coast was clear, he inched his way up the stairs. A piercing look from Juanita directed him to stay put, but he didn't heed the warning. She shook her head and waved her hand at him, "You gon get caught," she whispered.

Moe backed her into the corner of the porch, well out of Rudy's sight. He pulled her close and held her tightly in his arms.

"You sweaty." She tugged away.

"Awe, come heah, gal, to a real man."

She smiled at the crazy faces he was making and fell into his waiting embrace.

"I can't believe you asked Daddy if you could marry me."

Moe heaved his chest proudly, "Sho did, an' you heard him."

"Why you wanna marry me, Moe?" she asked, while peeking over his shoulder into the house.

"Cause you my girl, an' I don't wantcha roun' dat no good Harry Brown no mo, ya hea? And whatcha see in him anyway?"

"I don't know. What you want with dat Mary Jo?"

"I don't want no Mary Jo. Dat's ova. Dat's been ova. You my gal now."

"Well you betta hope it's ova. I heard she had dat nasty woman disease."

"What nasty woman disease?"

"The kine you ketch when you do the nasty."

Moe blurted out a loud laugh and Juanita slapped him in the mouth with the palm of her hand. "SHHHH! You gon make Daddy come back out heah...I hope you can run as fast as you say you can."

Moe giggled quietly and wrapped his lanky arms around her waist even tighter, "You don't have to worry about Mary Jo, Ms. Virgin."

"That's all right. You can pick all you want, but the Bible says save it for my husband and that's what I'm gon do. Save it," she remarked sarcastically.

"And who you saving it fo, me or Harry Brown?"

"Neither."

"Awe, hush, gal. You like'im cause he black as me, huh?"

"Who?"

"Harry Brown. I know ya like'im 'cause he dark jus' like me."

"There is plenty dark men roun' heah, Moe Jackson. I like'im cause he him, and I like you cause you, you."

Conceitedly, Moe stared down and said, "But you looove me."

The truth of the matter is that Juanita loved them both because they were so different. Moe was the rougher of the two. He didn't allow Juanita to get away with half the stuff Harry did. She loved a stern man, but Harry was affectionate and romantic. She loved that too. She figured that most stern men could not allow themselves to be romantic. At least that seemed to be Moe's case.

She laid the side of her head on his sweaty chest and closed her eyes. Lord, is this the man? I mean is this really the man you sent for me? The thought consumed her.

"Juanita," Moe tried to romantically whisper in her ear, "I don't want him roun' heah no mo. Every time I come ova heah, he heah. Every time I get somethin', he gotta get it too. Pisses me off. I get a outfit an' he gotta get that same outfit. I get a car an' he gotta get that same car."

"He got that car fo you did, Moe."

"Well, I thought of gettin' it first. I told Curtis I was thinkin' 'bout getting it, and I be damned if he didn't tell Harry. He only got it to show off to you."

"Oh, and you didn't?"

"Nope. Anyway, I don't see what you see in him. You know he seeing that Melba Jones ova in Bass County?"

"What?"

"Yep. You ain't heard? And I know you ain't gettin' mad, are ya?"

Juanita tried not to show it, but she was enraged at the thought of Harry Brown seeing another girl.

"I don't care."

"Well, since you don't care, I guess I'll finish telling ya. He was seen comin' out her house. Now I wonder what they was doin' in there?"

"Shut up, Moe Jackson. You wanna hold me or talk about Harry Brown all night?"

"All I'm sayin' is I bet not ketch him ova heah. When I see'im I'm gon tell'im not to come roun' heah no mo."

Juanita continued to snap at Moe for trying to dictate who could and could not come to her house, but she was really venting her anger at the thought of Harry seeing another girl.

Juanita pulled back from his arms and maneuvered her way out of the corner, "We ain't married yet, Moe Jackson. How you gon tell somebody not to come roun' heah? You don't tell nobody they can't come ova heah, this ain't yo house."

Moe reached out to grab her hand. She jerked back, banging her heel into the wooden stump that the Mason jar rested upon. It fell in slow motion, fragmenting in all directions. Rudy came dragging his way to the door.

"Nita,"

"Yes, Daddy."

"What's dat noise?"

"Awe, dis darn Mason jar fell off the stump and broke."

"Oh," Rudy looked around on the porch searching for Moe. "Where dat boy go?"

"Huh?"

When Moe first heard his voice, he took a giant leap, landing in half dirt and grass. He ran completely around the house back to his original spot.

"I'm right heah, sir," he said, out of breath and trying very hard not to sound like it. Rudy's eyes scanned the front yard.

"Where?"

"Right heah, sir."

Rudy's eyes searched through the dark, "Oh, there you are. You can stop smiling boy. I see ya." Rudy refused to move; he stood in the doorway listening.

"Well, I bess be goin' now," Moe announced when he realized Rudy wasn't budging from the screen door.

"Where ya going, Moe?"

"To the juke joint."

"You going to see dat Mary Jo, ain'tcha?"

"No, I ain't going to see no Mary Jo. I'm going to see if I can find Harry Brown."

"Fo what?"

"'Cause I wanna tell him we gittin' married."

"Well, I don't care where ya go," Rudy said, "but ya gotta get the hell away from heah wid all dat talk."

Moe made his way to his white Pontiac, started the engine and revved it several times before pulling off. His back wheels skidded loudly and he burned rubber turning the corner. In the distance, they could still hear the humming sound of the engine.

Rudy poked his head from behind the screen door like a turtle coming out of its shell. "They'll give anybody a damn license these days. I ain't never had a license, but I know I can drive better than that." As he withdrew his head, an identical white Pontiac pulled up close to the hedges in front of the house.

### III.

"Now, I know dat boy ain't been to the juke joint dat quick. What he want now?"

When Harry Brown skipped up the walkway, Juanita's eyes lit up like fireflies, with every tooth in her mouth shining in admiration.

"Dat ain't the same boy, is it?" asked Rudy, who squinted helplessly to observe the approaching face.

"Shhhh, Daddy."

Rudy watched through the screen door as Harry walked to the porch and rested his foot on the lower step. One would suppose that Rudy and Harry were best friends.

"Hey dar, Mr. Alexander."

Rudy stared at his foot, "Do I know you, boy?"

"Why, yes, sir, it's me, Harry Brown."

"I don't know you that well fo you to rest yo foot on my step."

"Oh, yes, sir." Quickly Harry Brown moved his foot. "This was a pretty day, wouldn't you say, sir?"

Rudy came from within the house, "Too hot. Heat like dis give me a rash."

Juanita listened and continued to grin. Her eyes flowed over Harry Brown's pinstriped suit down to his Stacey Adams shoes. His hair was permed and pressed on the sides. The darkness of his skin, mixed with the deep color of his hair, created a richness that even a chocolate bar couldn't replicate.

That's one fine man, she thought.

"You just comin' from a funeral, boy?"

"No, sir."

"Why you got on all that black fo?" Rudy asked, cautiously dragging his stiff leg over to the rocking chair.

"I just got out of church. A pastor from out of town came in." Harry Brown clapped his hands together, "Lord knows that man could preach. Praise the Lord."

"Uh huh, is that right?" sighed Rudy. "Nita," he called, "get me another drink."

"I'll be right back, Brown," she said, vanishing into the house.

Juanita liked the idea of combining Moe's first name with Harry's last name. When anyone asked whom she was dating, she would simply say, "Moe Brown," but nobody in the county had ever heard of Moe Brown. That was the way she liked it, and that was the only way she could have them both without either one complaining about the other. She knew it wasn't right to lead two men on, but she couldn't figure out why God sent her two men to love. It didn't make sense to her. She knew that God had the answer, but she just had to be patient enough to wait on it. Harry waited until Juanita was out of sight before speaking to Rudy.

"Mr. Alexander, sir, I'm glad we can have dis time alone, sir, because there is something I been meaning to ask you. Now, you know I'm very fond of your dauder."

"You are?" asked Rudy.

"Why, yes, sir, I am. I wish your permission to have her hand in marriage."

"Is that right?" Rudy questioned as he lifted his feet onto the banister. "And why should she have you?"

Brown spoke articulately and with poise, "For several reasons, sir. I'm in the church; I'm educated; and I will have a good paying job. There ain't a doubt in my mind I can give her the life she wants and deserves, sir."

"You ain't got a job now?"

"No, sir, but I plan on gettin' one."

"Well, what you do now?"

"Nothin' really, sir."

"Yeah, I bet you good at dat."

Rudy looked on, giving no approving reaction. All he cared about was who would make Juanita happy. According to Rudy, some of the biggest devils were in the church camouflaged as sheep. And far as he was concerned, Juanita had already picked, and this boy was just a little too late.

"Nita," cried Rudy.

Juanita hurried onto the porch with another full jar of homemade brandy and a great big smile. "Huh, Daddy."

Rudy didn't wait, "Dis boy heah say he want to marry ya."

Juanita stood there with her mouth gaping. Her body grew completely numb.

Lord, what are you doing to me? she thought.

"Gal, you hear me?" Rudy repeated, "this boy," using the jar as a pointing tool, "want to know if he can marry you." For a brief moment, it appeared that Rudy grinned. "Well, go on and answer him."

Harry lowered to one knee, "Juanita, I love ya and I want to marry ya."

Still Juanita said nothing.

"Juanita, you do know I love you, don't ya? What fool 'sides me would get on his knees beggin' in front'a yo daddy?"

Rudy interrupted, "G'on and tell'im 'bout the other fool..." Juanita cut Rudy off, "I want Brown, Daddy," she replied.

"What!? Now you jus' said you want dat otha Negro."

"Daddy, I want Brown."

"Well, make up yo mind, gal! If ya wanted dis boy you shouldna told the otha one ya wanted him. I told ya I'm tireda all dese different Negroes comin' to my house. I don't wanna see no mo boys in front of my house startin' tonight. Else I'm gon get to shooting. Now you figure out what you gon do."

## IV.

Brown stood at the bottom of the stairs with his hands in his pockets, "So am I to take it you promised Moe yo hand in marriage?"

"Well... I don't know."

Brown leaned forward, caught the pupils of Rudy's eyes and insisted, "I don't plan on giving up without a fight." Juanita knew that he meant every word he said, and that was the last thing she needed.

A thunderous roar echoed from the street corner throughout the entire block. Moe Jackson pulled his white Pontiac around the corner so fast that he smashed right into the back of Brown's car, BAM, and knocked it out of gear. It rolled several feet and hit the light post in front of the house. Rudy jumped up and pulled his pistol as Moe climbed from behind the wheel of the car.

"I knew it!" he yelled from the street. "You sneakin' down heah to see my fiancée, you no good dirty dog."

"Your fiancée?" Brown screamed back. He positioned himself in a fighting stance. Moe made his way into the yard and walked directly over to Brown. They stood face to face, eyeing one another. Rudy shook the gun at the two of them. "I ain't having it! Not heah," he yelled. "So bof'a y'all get the hell out my yard."

71

Brown spoke, "Sir, this nigga done wrecked the back of my car! Lord, forgive me, but he got to catch an ass whipping heah today."

"If you think you man enough to give it to me then let's do it."

The two grabbed and tugged each other until Rudy leaned over the banister, cocked the gun and pointed it directly at them. They froze immediately.

"Now I said get outta my yard."

"I ain't leavin' 'til he leave," shouted Brown.

"Dis my fiancée he sneakin' down heah to see," screamed Moe.

"How can she be your fiancée when she jus' said she gon marry me?" replied Brown.

"She ain't nobody's fiancée," Rudy yelled. "I got two bullets—one for each of ya, and if ya don't get out my damn yard, they gon marry you right in yo a..."

"Daddy," screamed Juanita.

The two boys still didn't budge.

"Nita," Rudy yelled, "I told you to decide which one ya wanted. Here they are, now pick!"

Juanita said nothing for several minutes. Her eyes volleyed from one to the other as she stood there in confusion. "Daddy, I don't know which one I want. As soon as I think the Lord dun told me, he come sendin' me another. I'm as confused as a chicken with his head cut off. My mind is goin' in all directions. Daddy, I'm waiting on the Lord to tell me."

"Well, you betta tell the Lord to hurry up and make a house call, or else these two Negroes is gon be callin' on Him."

"Daddy, I love'em both. Lord, please send me a sign."

She covered her face with both hands as Rudy continued to scold, "Whatcha doin' messin' with two men at one time anyway? Didn't I raise you better? I know ya grown, but as long as ya livin' with me ya gon live by my rules. Now it's only one man gon be at my house besides me, and dat's the one ya marry."

Brown tossed his hand in the air and interrupted, "Mr. Alexander, sir. I might have a solution to all of our problems."

"What kinda solution?" asked Moe.

"Shut up boy and let me hear what this boy gotta say."

"Well, sir, you want Juanita to decide right now on who she want. Now I just be willing to wait on the Lord to send her a sign." He turned and looked at Moe, "Personally I think He already has. He brought me in her life."

"Boy, I don't have all night tryin' to figure out what you talking 'bout, so make some sense of what you saying."

"Yeah. Make some sense, boy," repeated Moe.

"Anyhow, I know a prophet who can tell people certain things about their life. Give them direction, sir. He is anointed by God. Sir, I'm sure he can help Juanita decide which man she oughta marry."

"Juanita don't need no root doctor tellin' her what man she should marry. I can tell her dat. I am the man," Moe was putting up a fight.

"Negro, please," Brown said, "this man ain't no root doctor. He is an anointed man of God."

Rudy was thinking while Moe and Brown argued amongst themselves.

"Both of y'all shut up! Now where you say dis man live?"

"At the edge of town, sir."

Moe had to speak up, "Sir, you don't want him takin' yo dauder to some stranger. He probably some chicken-eating preacher who only visits on Sundays, licking his chops."

"Mr. Alexander, bein' dat you want her to decide and all, and bein' dat she can't do it on her own, maybe God can give the prophet a sign." Brown directed his next comment to Moe, "Now if you got a better solution, then tell us."

"Yeah, I got a betta solution. You can leave and I can stay."

"Sir, this is your decision," Brown said, then looked at Juanita as she pulled her hands down from her face.

"Daddy, I don't know. I am Baptist. I ain't never been to no prophet." She turned toward Brown, "I always been told prophets don't exist today."

"That's what your religion says," replied Brown.

"Well, my preacher says to be patient and continue to pray about it."

"And I agree. But your father wants a decision now."

"I dun run out of patience, gal. Now either you can go see this man or you can say bye to both of them right now."

Juanita's head dropped and her eyes followed the cracks along the wooden porch.

"Well, gal?"

"OK, Daddy."

With an irate look, Rudy pointed to Brown, "Now since you told me about this man, I hold my dauder in yo care. If anything happen to her, don't come back."

Moe smiled and agreed, "Yeah, don't come back."

Rudy's glare cut its way sharply to Moe, "And don't you come back neither."

## V.

The three of them stood beneath a dim lamppost directly across the street from the prophet's house. Moe and Brown took their positions on each side of Juanita, both claiming their territory by grabbing her hand.

"Look, y'all, stop for a minute," Juanita said. "We come for a reason."

"I'm walkin' ya up there," Moe demanded, pulling her to him.

Brown jerked her by the other arm, "Allow some class to walk her."

"Take that process out yo head, den let's see how much class you got."

"Stop, y'all!" pleaded Juanita, "before ya pull my arms off."

The two squared off.

"I'll go by myself. I'm the one who got to see him. So y'all stay right heah."

Her eyes followed the long flight of steps that led to the front porch. Moe and Brown had spaced themselves a few feet apart, but still within the path of the light.

"I want you to know when she decide on me, I don't want you comin' roun' her no mo, ya hea?" said Moe.

"And the same for you," replied Brown.

When Juanita reached the front porch, an old pale-faced man opened the door.

"Come in, my child," he said.

His voice was soft and pleasant—almost hypnotizing. He turned to head down a long foyer when Juanita spoke up, "Sir, I bess tell ya now why I've come. My daddy wants me to decide what man I should marry."

The elderly man turned to the left of the foyer and entered an adjoining room.

"Sit down, my child, and relax yourself," he directed. Juanita passed a window that overlooked the street. Moe and Brown were sitting on opposite sides of the pole, batting away the attacking mosquitoes and gnats.

"My child, I don't believe God chooses husbands or wives for us so that later when things don't work out, we can blame Him. He places people in our paths and allows us to make wise or unwise decisions. He guides us, yes. Through processes, we remove what is not best for us; that is if we are listening to Him and all that He has taught us. You have to trust Him to lead you in the right direction."

"That's what I thought I was doin', but my daddy wants me to pick now."

"Let me pray for you child. Learn to trust God and everything will be ok."

Juanita was watchful as the man placed both of her hands on the table. Reaching over to the dresser, he got a bottle of olive oil. He rubbed a couple of drops in his hands, then placed a few drops into the palms of her hands and on her forehead. As he began to pray over her, Juanita listened and faded into a conversation of her own with the Lord.

*Lord, I'm so nervous. I'm not scared, but I can't wait. Part of me wants you to pick Moe and the other part wants Brown. But Lord let your will be done.* Suddenly she was filled with a cold excitement. *Oh no, Lord, don't choose either. I mean, do choose one,* she pleaded. She could barely wait for the prophet to finish praying. *God, I'm so glad I'm not in your shoes.*

Her face frowned with curiosity. All she wanted was an answer. Then his eyes opened and he stated, "My child, God gave me a word to give you."

"He did?"

"Yes. Know the tree by the fruit it bears."

"Well, what does that mean?"

The prophet tried to explain in a simpler manner, "Don't marry the darkest."

"What? I should do what?"

"Do not marry the darkest," the prophet repeated. He then rose from the table and headed back towards the foyer. Juanita hadn't moved from the table. She was even more confused now than before she came.

Once in the foyer, he waved for her to accompany him.

"Sir, is that the Lord's sign? His answer is for me not to marry the darkest one? Doesn't the Lord realize they both are dark? He must know," she said, "that one is as black as tar and the other one is black as coal. He made them, so he must know."

She pulled back from the table and entered the foyer where the prophet stood. "I don't know who is the darkest or the lightest. All I know is that my daddy said pick one. And he is so tired of them bickerin' and bristlin' at each other. He wants an answer, and he wants an answer tonight. How am I supposed to go back and tell him, 'The Lord says for me not to marry the darkest one'? My daddy gon think I lost my everlasting mind. Part of me thinks I have."

The prophet placed a hand on her shoulder and said comfortingly, "My child, the Lord will never place a burden on you that you can't handle."

"Don't marry the darkest. You don't think that's more than I can handle?"

When the prophet opened the door, both Moe and Brown were still sitting at the light post. They rose to their feet. The prophet stared down at the two men who waited at attention by the pole.

"You see my problem now, Mister? How am I supposed to choose who is the lightest? They are the same complexion?"

"Yes, I see your dilemma, now, and why you're confused, but maybe the Lord is revealing to you that both trees are bearing similar fruit."

"Oh, Lord," shouted Juanita.

"What is it, child?"

"It's been revealed to me three times."

"Three times?"

"Yes, I missed the revelation twice." She thought back to what her father said about wolves in sheep's clothing, and her recent prayer in the prophet's house.

# BLACK MEN,
# KEEP YOUR VOWS

## I.

Her hair was a dirty brown that extended up from the roots of her head and sprouted about as wild alfalfa in a distant field. Her body bore all the woes that any woman could have. The silhouette of her frame danced on and off the wall as she moved ever so gently across one side of the small, squeaky, antique bed.

She was beautiful, even though time had blessed her generously in certain spots. A number of dark rings dipped around and under her eyes, camouflaging not one beauty mark.

Isley had seen her like this many times before, many times. After a long time staring at the wall, she grabbed Irvin's poem. It was her poem that she wrote the first time they met.

> *"Dear butterfly, my butterfly,*
> *will you pass me by*
> *or are we compatible*
> *like you and the sky*
> *in which you fly so high*
> *my beautiful, colorful butterfly..."*

Two moves and a fire had effaced the rest of the poem. It was amazing that the poem still existed, so old and wrinkled; a ring of stain from years of dust and water covered its paper. She folded the poem and stuffed it into an old box along with other wrinkled papers, and away under the bed it went.

"JACQUE!!!"

It was Irvin. His deep baritone voice echoed throughout the house and searched her out. Jacque lay on the bed, eyes closed as though she were dead,

dead and gone to God's world where no pain exists. Isley was in the closet watching her every move, trying to feel what she was feeling.

"Where are you, Jacque?"

She didn't answer, she just lay there with her eyes tightly closed. Irvin always called her Jacque, short for Jacqueline. She was named by her grandmother after First Lady Jacqueline Kennedy. During that time, it was rare that blacks were taught about black heroes or black role models, so it was an honor to be named after the first lady.

As he climbed the stairs, the thud of stomps accompanied his loud calling. Isley listened as Irvin's heavy feet struck each step. Usually the wood let off a soft squeak, but this time it sounded hollow. Before Irvin reached the top of the stairs, Isley had managed to crawl his way to the front of the closet. He slowly pushed the door open and positioned himself behind a box of old clothes.

"Jacque, didn't you hear me?" He waited in the doorway for an answer.

The light from an antique lamp, whose shade was filled with small holes, lit a portion of the room. When she rose from the bed, her body formed a silhouette upon the wall. Her eyes focused on his image, but not completely.

Isley knew it was coming and began to whisper like many times before. "Oh! Daddy, please don't beat Momma. Please, Daddy." His eyes filled with tears as he looked on.

When they first got married, devoted to true love and the sacred vows they made to God, they wanted nothing less than a perfect family—a family with two or three kids like the ones seen in movies. It seemed so possible in the beginning.

Isley watched quietly from the closet. Unlike other wives who stayed with their abusive husbands for a sense of security, Jacque stayed because she took an oath to her Lord and Savior, her kids, and her husband. " 'Til death us do part."

She could feel the pain as she curled up along the bed rail, even before he got there. It was only a moment later that the blood and mucous tried to mix, tangled just like the vows of their marriage and trying desperately to get themselves apart because they, too, did not mix. Yet her fear and his control were powerful enough forces to keep the two of them together.

Isley screamed as his mother's head collided with the wall. Suddenly her silhouette, cast from the beauty of her image, was ruined when traces of blood splattered upon her shadow. Isley's eyes and shoulders inched upward, tightening as each blow sounded louder and louder. The struggle of their breaths clashed, one trying to free herself as prey and the other to capture and kill as predator. As she could do no more than grab a pillow to protect herself from the other blows, Isley screamed and retreated quickly to the back of the closet behind other boxes of old clothes. Nothing made him hate his father more.

Irvin swung open the closet door and jerked Isley by his arm. "Isley, get yo ass out of there! How many times have I told ya not to come in this room...huh, boy?"

Isley's first inclination was to fight his father, just to fight someone—anyone. The hate built as he glanced upon the weeping eyes of his mother. They were filled with pain from years of mental and physical abuse. Each teardrop was another promise unfulfilled by Irvin. But Isley saw something deeper in his mother's eyes through all the tears and pain. He saw the disgust she felt for his father, yet, the deeper thing was her lack of disownership.

The shortness of her breath followed Isley out of the room and her whining like a baby reminded him of himself—all cried out because of the word "no." Now she, too, pleads no. No more beatings, no more fussing and confusion, no more abuse.

Isley turned in the hall and watched through the small opening in the door. Irvin was trying to comfort Jacque, stroking her soft, dirty, brown hair. "I'm sorry, I'm sorry, baby," he said over and over. Just another sorry added to thousands of sorries, redundant as the thousand beatings he so spontaneously had given.

## II.

The room was cold and dim. The only light was from the street light on the corner, lighting just a small portion of the room. Isley searched in the dark for an extra pair of socks; color was of no importance even in the daylight. The important thing was keeping warm. He slipped off the old, raggedy All Stars that his mother had purchased at a yard sale and pulled the other pair of socks over the already worn socks on his feet. It was getting colder and the autumn breeze would set in fast, putting a chill on the house. With a lack of money for fuel, this winter was going to be rough. Isley stood in the middle of the

floor shivering and thinking. His fear that he could
be like his father scared him more than the meanest
bully, the thought of being poor, or even dying. Cold
air seeped through the windowsill and broke his concentration, while the cold from the wooden floor penetrated through the two pairs of socks. After stuffing
several dirty shirts in front of the window to stop
the incoming air, he demanded Irene and Isaac to
move over in the bed. He was older, so they had no
choice. The three of them lay down to sleep in a small
bed hardly big enough for two. They curled up one
beside the other, refusing to separate their bodies,
which supplied a sufficient amount of warmth underneath the knitted wool blanket, restitched many
times over.

It was so warm, the sun on his face and his skin
soaking up all its rays. Isley was dreaming, the place
where he often went day and night. At this place
he knew there would be no arguing or fighting, just
pleasant thoughts and happiness. What more could a
thirteen-year-old ask for?

Isley balled more into his knot, tucking additional cover under himself as though it were sand.
Out of the knot, his lanky legs stretched the entire
length of the bed. Still dreaming and disturbing no
one, he poured his tropical drink over his head to
cool himself. It ran down his full cheeks and curled
under his chin like a stream of tears, then continued down his predeveloped pectorals and along his
thighs. It felt so cool, so refreshing, and so real. With
a stroke of his fingers, he wiped up a bit of the remaining flow and proceeded to glide his fingers over

his tongue. What he hoped would be a sweet, fruity nectar, brewed to create the perfect taste, was instead sharp, pungent, bitter, and brewed from the bowels of his sister.

"Irene, get up!" Isley yelled in anger like his father, but he couldn't move.

"You don peed in the bed again." Isley spat and rubbed his tongue on his sleeve and spat again trying to get rid of that awful taste. "I'm tired of you peeing on me!"

As he threw back the knitted blanket, an acrid smell of urine along with a puff of warm steam greeted him. "Momma! Momma, Irene don peed in the bed again."

Isaac, the second oldest child, didn't seem to mind as long as he was warm, and such heat was welcomed as he curled up in the yellow, wet warmth, grabbing for more cover.

## III.

There was something about the morning breakfast that could calm even the wildest beast. Jacque stood in the kitchen over the stove scrambling the few eggs they had left and frying the remaining bacon. Vents open in the floor allowed the aroma of bacon, eggs, and sausage to flow throughout the house, filling all of their noses and, like zombies, they rose out of bed. The house was cold and Isley, Irene, and Isaac searched for warm clean clothes. They hurried when they smelled the fresh-baked bread. Jacque had fixed the type of homemade bread that cracks on the surface letting out just a little steam—enough to tantalize you until you break it apart yourself. And the heat from the oven kept the kitchen warm. She always left the oven door open to heat the kitchen.

"Momma," his voice was calmer than before. "Irene don peed in the bed again and I had planned on wearing these pants to school today."

"How many times have I told you not to wear your clothes to bed?"

"But, Momma, it was cold."

"Go on up stairs and take them clothes off," she said, pulling the sheet pan filled with bacon out of the oven.

She directed her attention towards Irene who was in the doorway sucking her thumb and shivering. "Get that thumb out yo mouth girl and help me set this table. You're seven years old now and it's time for you to start helping momma." Jacque looked down at Irene's pajamas. "Are those pajamas wet?"

"No, ma'am. I slept in my nightgown."

"But your underwear is wet?"

"I changed those too."

"Now I know you haven't washed up. After you set the table, go back upstairs and change the sheets and wash up. Isaac, go back and take those pissy draws off and wash up."

Jacque watched as Irene set the table; she was too tired to reset the knives and the forks. Instead she turned and stood over the boiling water and allowed the steam to fill her nostrils and water her eyes. She was sore and tired. Irvin had bruised her ribs and caused her jaw to swell. And the makeup she used could not disguise the red and purple discoloration.

Isley came running back down the steps, skipping the last few. His feet slammed on the floor.

Jacque popped her head around the corner. "Boy, are you crazy? Stop all that noise. Is your father awake?"

He shook his head no and walked softly towards her.

"Go down to the basement and get some coal."

"Why I got to get it? I always get it," he frowned.

Jacque gave him one of those looks that didn't need an explanation.

"Yes, ma'am."

"Isaac, did you hear me? Get on up them steps and take them wet clothes off."

"Huh?"

"Boy, I know you are not trying me early this morning."

She grabbed him by the arm and pushed him toward the staircase. "And wake yo daddy up."

Isley returned with a tin bucket of coal and dumped it into the mouth of an old beat-up wood stove in the corner of the room. He grabbed a few brown paper bags, crumpled and stuffed them into the mouth of the stove. Only a tittle of oil was left in a small can sitting behind the stove. He squeezed the thin aluminum can over the coal and brown bags until it was empty. After striking a match several times, it finally lit. Stepping away from the stove, he tossed it in. WOOOOOSH!!!! Flames came roaring out at him. Isley closed the mouth of the stove and stood as close as he possibly could without getting burned. He hugged the stove, refusing to leave its side, knowing that just a step or two away the cold air was waiting.

Isaac ran down the stairs and joined Isley by the stove. The warmth had seduced the two of them. Irvin was awake and Jacque gave a quick motion with her head for the two of them to get into the kitchen. Irvin entered the room. The sides of his hair were flat and nappy. He had not even taken the time to get the sleep out of his eyes. Still hung over from last night, and like all mornings after an abusive night, he seemed not to remember. His voice was low and groggy as he growled a good morning. Everyone replied except Isley, who saw him as the king of hypocrites.

"Mm, Mm, Mm, baby this smells good," Irvin said as he proceeded to grab one of the crisp slices of bacon that was about to fall off the plate.

"Don't you dare touch that bacon, Irvin Michael Harmon. Isley, get your baby sister a bib."

It was amazing, thought Isley, how his mother could so defend grace but not her dignity, so defend Irvin but not herself, so defend his forgotten vows of marriage and adhere to her own. He bent to place the bib around his fifteen-month-old sister. As he looked up, he could not help but notice the bruises on his father's knuckles. Isley clinched his teeth and took his place at the table. They all bowed their heads to pray.

# AS I STOOD AT THE GATE

## END OF SUMMER, 1965

10:00 a.m.
Saturday Morning

Matilean Johnson stood on the street corner staring at Old Man Woodson's house. With one hand twirling an extended pigtail, she spat on the other and caressed the saliva over her ashy, skinny legs. She possessed the complexion of dark mocha mixed with midnight. She adjusted her blouse and straightened her black mini-skirt. A few specks of dust had collected on the patent-leather shoes she wore only on special occasions. With a quick brush of her hand and a few wipes around the soles, the dust was gone. She wanted to look nothing less than perfect. Contemplative, once again, her gaze fell upon the house.

*Old Man Woodson lived in a beautiful house at the edge of a historic district in Lynchburg, Virginia. For fifteen years he took care of the grounds of the sixteen-room house for Mr. O'Neal, a rich, white banker. The house had been in Mr. O'Neal's family for over a half century, and while other families sold their properties because of the fuel shortage during World War II, Mr. O'Neal held on to his home. As fuel was rationed, and as it became too expensive to keep up these large homes, more families began to abandon them. Many of these abandoned homes endured seasons of bad weather and no maintenance. Realtors found it very lucrative to restructure and renovate many of these beautiful, dilapidated homes into small apartments. Working, middle-class whites moved in and occupied the majority of the apartments and single-family homes. But it wasn't until the Negro population began renting in the historic district that Mr. O'Neal, too, chose to take refuge in a white, affluent, suburban neighborhood. Rather than sell his beautiful home to the realtors, he sold the entire property to Old Man Woodson and at a poor man's price.*

*Mr. O'Neal was amazed by how much Old Man Woodson resembled a white man, given his straight hair, blue eyes, pointed nose, and thin lips. He became very fond of Old Man Woodson and treated him just like a brother, the brother he never had. He introduced him to friends at the all-white country club, shared many late afternoon drinks on the porch, and confided in him. It was no secret that Old Man Woodson acquired the property because of the complexion of his skin and not his labor.*

Matilean approached the black handrail that ran alongside rock steps in front of Old Man Woodson's house. The rocks ended two feet in front of a beautifully wired, green gate. On each side of the gate were flower hedges that ran along each side of the house. Matilean leaned on the gate to peek around one of the hedges for a better look at the front yard. In opposite corners of the yard were two pine trees. A concrete walkway led from the gate to the bottom of the porch stairs and continued around the right side of the house. Another black handrail divided the flight of red steps that led to the porch. On each side of the steps was a flat stoop, most often used for placing potted arrangements, but sometimes used for sitting. The house had a high, black, L-shaped porch outlined with a white picket banister attached by tall, white pillars. A garden of roses, lilacs, and tulips hid the contents under the porch. The house was white with windows perfectly trimmed in green. What a beautiful house, she thought. How could black folks afford such a house?

As she stood quietly on one of the rock steps in front of the green, wired gate, she settled deeper into thought, not allowing the tears to cascade down her cheeks. She brought to mind the first time she really saw the gate; its twisted structure coincided with her mother's fears and Old Man Woodson's threats that she didn't belong there.

When Matilean and Seth weren't physically meeting, Matilean was mentally spending every minute of the day with him. It was the one afternoon when Seth didn't appear that forced her by his house. His promises encouraged her to approach his gate, and the thought of his awaiting embrace magnetized her feet to proceed beyond the boundary of the gate.

The voice of distress tested his devotion. And his family values denied her the opportunity to greet him like a beautiful, summer breeze coming in from the south. Surprisingly to Matilean, Seth's voice rushed off the porch with abrupt anxiety, and a tornado of panic blew his summer breeze off course. The truth of her status and his position was revealed at the gate on that day.

The events of that day solidified suspicions her mother embraced about fair-skinned people. For Matilean, somehow the gate mimicked her life: iron that was forced together by a continuous twist was enough to hold the gate together; but Matilean wasn't sure of the amount of strength it would take to hold her together.

"Get offa Daddy's gate!" a voice shouted from the porch.

Matilean paid no attention because that voice sounded like a familiar foe. As she started out that morning, she had decided that no obstacle would deter her—she was on a mission. She turned her head to peek at the sun behind her. "Whew, it's gon be a scorcher," she mumbled.

A few drops of sweat ran from her neck all the way down the center of her back. It had to be settled today, she demanded to herself, slicing her index finger through the air. She couldn't take any more; the worries had damn near driven her crazy. It was just too much pressure for her to endure. Nervously, she swayed from side to side, talking to herself while steadily shaking her finger in the air.

"I got to be direct, firm, and in control," she mumbled again. "I can't let his pretty hazel eyes get the best of me. No more tomorrow or later on, it's today! That's right, today!"

Again a voice screamed from the porch, "I said get yo black hands offa my daddy's gate!"

For a brief moment she thought it might be Old Man Woodson, but then she realized it really was Lillian, Old Man Woodson's youngest daughter.

Lillian stood on the edge of the porch and looked down at Matilean. The height of the porch allowed her to feel superior. No bigger than her bark, Lillian was small in stature and big in mouth. Silky, black hair hung below her buttocks. She favored Old Man Woodson with her thick eyebrows that met to form a unibrow. The Irish in her blood was obvious from her high cheekbones and stern chin. The two began a stare-off that lasted for several minutes.

Matilean began having doubts about being there. "No, you can't run away. You here now," she murmured.

"Girl, I know you heard me. Back offa Daddy's gate." Lillian placed her hands on her hips and then shifted her weight from one side to the other.

Matilean stared smugly. She had heard this all before from Lillian at school—running off at the mouth but saying nothing of importance.

"Whatcha doin' comin' 'round here? This ain't yo neighbahood. You know Daddy don't like yo type."

She considered entertaining Lillian's childish remark.

"And what type would that be?" Matilean asked, as she purposely placed her hands on the gate to irritate Lillian.

"You know what type I'm talkin' 'bout. Ain't no need in ackin' all dumb."

"Where is yo brotha, Lilly?"

"Lookin' for Seth, huh, and what for?"

"That's nunna yo business. Is he heah or not?"

"Oh, he's heah, but I ain't gettin'im." Lillian stepped down to the top red step. "Go on home blackie! I dun told you Daddy don't want yo kind 'round heah. You make the property depreciate."

Matilean hated that she had a low tolerance for people like Lillian. It just meant trouble. What she wouldn't give to punch Lillian right in the mouth. She figured that would shut her up, at least for the moment. She gave Lillian a false grin as if the comment had no effect on her.

"Well, you know what they say Lilly, the blacka the berry, the sweeta the juice. Ask yo brotha."

"I'll tell you what they say, 'the lighta the honey sucka, the betta the necta'."

It was obvious that Lillian was looking for a fight, and she was barking up just the right tree. Although her sweet disposition could fool you, Matilean was skilled in the art of fighting. Being the youngest of three sisters and a brother, she learned quickly. You want a fight, huh? Then I'll give you a fight, thought Matilean, as her grip tightened around the top of the gate. Her jaw imprint bulged as she bit down on her teeth. She had very little patience left for this bantering.

"Nothin' to say, spook?" continued Lillian.

"Yeah, come on out heah. I wanna tell ya in yo face." Matilean hoped Lillian would accept her offer.

"Naw, tell me from here, darkie." Lillian was no fool.

"Well, the darka the skin, the deepa the roots," replied Matilean, now waiting for retaliation. Lillian skipped to the bottom of the steps.

Yeah, come on a bit closer and you'll be in reach, thought Matilean. To Matilean's misfortune, Lillian stopped just out of reach.

"Darka the gal, nappia the hair," replied Lillian, while rolling her eyes.

"Lilly, you gon always be a runner-up to me. You nothin' but half-breed, white trash. You hate the fact that this dark...beautiful...black skin can turn the head of the finest man. So be intimidated 'cause if you don't watch it, I might take yo man."

"No you don't, heifer," Lillian shouted. That did it! Lillian's blushed complexion had now turned a dark mauve and before she knew it, her finger was right in Matilean's face.

"That's exactly what I wanted you to do," grunted Matilean, when she grabbed Lillian's finger and pulled her closer. She frowned and then yanked a chunk of Lillian's long, pretty, black hair.

"Let go! Let go of my hair!"

With all of her strength, Lillian tried to pull away, but Matilean held on tight. Lillian defiantly screamed and yelled for Matilean to let go of her hair. Lillian didn't know enough about Matilean to say something that would send her into one of her awkward daydreams, but when Lillian's face turned with pity before softly saying, "Matilean, please don't hit me," Matilean slipped into her thoughts.

Matilean's mother was quick to dispel the daydreams as unnatural; she believed the daydreams made Matilean appear crazy. "It just ain't right," her mother would say, "fo a girl to be talkin' at one minute or doin' somethin', and then disappear into her mind the next minute."

The thought of what Christ would do, a phrase her mother often used, leaped out in her daydream and pierced her heart. Now was not the time for mercy, she thought. Yet, something within her inner core was overriding her thoughts and she began to loosen her grip around Lillian's hair. Lillian, however, wasn't patient enough to wait for Matilean to completely release her grip.

"Let go of me now, you Black Aunt Jemima!"

At that moment Matilean drew her fist back in the air and bit down harder on her teeth.

"BANG!"

The screen door slammed in the front of the house. Old Man Woodson and Seth scuffled onto the porch. Quickly, Matilean released Lillian's hair and they both dropped to the ground on either side of the gate. The two girls knelt in silence, their fingers laced over one another's as they clung to the gate.

Old Man Woodson ran his house like he was running a prison. He stood 6 feet 4 inches, and carried 255 pounds of solid muscle. From the stories Seth had told Matilean, she knew Old Man Woodson had to be the meanest man alive. There was never any evidence to prove otherwise. Old Man Woodson frowned continuously. His eyes were cold and menacing, frequently moving from one direction to another as he contemplated what punishment he would inflict upon the next infractor.

Seth's upper torso limply extended over the banister, supported only by his father's firm grip around his neck. Seth's complexion went from a light red to a deep purple. Old Man Woodson wouldn't let go. Instead, he gripped tighter, cutting off more oxygen. Pounding down on his father's forearm, Seth tried to free himself from the grasp, but to no avail. Old Man Woodson's face tightened. His lips pressed into his gums and his eyes squinted with vengeance. Seth literally tried spitting out words.

"Pl...e...a...s...e. I...ccccccan'...t...Bre..."

"Ah know you can't breathe! You can't breathe 'cause Ah'm chokin' you, you damn fool!" Old Man Woodson yelled.

Finally, he pulled Seth's limp body back onto the porch. Seth collapsed to his knees, fighting to catch his breath.

"What? You tryin' to kill me?" he asked, gasping for as much air as he could. Strings of saliva hung from his mouth to the surface of the black porch.

"If dat's whut it takes," his voice still cold. "Boy, don't you eva," he stressed his words, "come in my face wid some shit like that. You see any dark women in this family?" He answered for Seth, "Naw, and will neva be if I got anythin' to say to the matta!"

Seth snorted up the remaining snot that hung from his upper lip. He lifted himself to face his father. Their physiques were identical.

"What differ does it matter?" Seth questioned, backing up after he asked.

"Whut, boy?" screamed Old Man Woodson.

Seth's disrespectful reply was enough to make Old Man Woodson's eyes cringe with anger. His big, wide hand came descending through the air. With one blow, Seth's body crashed into the banister. A second slap was in motion.

"NOOOO! Daddy," Lillian cried.

Her body was crunched into the gate and her hands clenched Matilean's. For the first time, Old Man Woodson took notice of Lillian and Matilean kneeling at the gate. Trickles of blood dripped from Seth's nose and landed in the puddle of saliva. Matilean watched as the blood and the saliva mixed on the porch floor. Without order or control, Matilean slipped into another thought. How strange it seemed to her that something as black as the porch and something as clear as saliva could still find the color of blood.

"How long you been there?" Old Man Woodson yelled, as he walked to the edge of the porch.

He stood tall like a giant and more intimidating to Matilean than Lillian could have ever been.

"Did you hea me? How long you been there?"

Lillian spoke up quickly, "We ain't been here long, Daddy."

Old Man Woodson's attention was directed solely to Matilean. He waited for her to answer. Matilean came out of her thought in time to hear Old Man Woodson say, "You hea whut I said, gal?"

"No, we ain't heard nothin', Daddy," Lillian answered.

"Lilly."

"Yes, Daddy."

"Am Ah talkin' to you?"

She pondered a second. "Ummmm no, Daddy."

"Then speak when spoken to. Betta yet, come heah," he demanded.

As Lillian began to stand, Matilean clutched her fingers tighter. All the hurtful words spoken earlier were trivial now, as destruction seemed to lie in their path. Matilean wanted to protect her and the innocence that was underneath her cold and bitter facade.

Lillian reluctantly pulled her fingers away and walked very slowly towards the steps and even more slowly up them.

"Get in the house!" he insisted by grabbing her around the neck and spinning her towards the screen door. He never took his eyes off Matilean the entire time.

Matilean heard exactly what he said, but she was scared to answer him. If he choked his own kids, she could only imagine what he wanted to do to her neck.

"Well, gal," repeated Old Man Woodson.

At that moment, Matilean noticed a robin singing in one of the pine trees. She wondered why it
sang, because there seemed to be nothing exciting
to sing about. Even a caged bird with its door open
wouldn't sing at a time like this.

Softly she spoke, allowing her eyes to rise to his
waist and fall back to the ground.

"I didn't hear nothing, sir."

"Well, betta you did, but since you didn't, Ah'll
be glad to say it again. Don't expect to be in this family. Ain't one of ya eva been in this family, and it'll be
ova my dead body if one of ya eva is. Don't make no
diffa nohow. Seth be goin' to war any day now. He
got his papers, so whateva you plannin', get it on out
yo head. And anotha thing, don't eva let me catch
you pass that gate." He turned to Seth. "Clean yoself
up, boy," and then he disappeared into the house,
slamming the screen door behind him.

His words hovered in the air. Matilean slowly
rose to her feet. She knew she would never forget
that day. Matilean was proud of Seth. How she loved
him for standing up to his father and for her. Never
had she imagined he would do such a thing. Most
of the guys she knew were childish. She couldn't afford having a boy right now; she needed a man. She
needed Seth.

"I'm proud of you, Seth," she said, pausing. "It
took a brave man to even think about standin' up to
yo father. You actually did it. You tellin'im sho took a
weight off my shoul...."

"I didn't tell'im," Seth interrupted.

"Whatcha mean you didn't tell'im? I heard you
tell'im."

"Naw, you kinda heard me tell'im."

"Well, whatcha tell'im to make him darn near strangle the life out of you?"

Seth paused, his eyes in a daze. "I told'im I wanted to make you my girl."

"WHAT!" screamed Matilean.

Forget the fact that Old Man Woodson might hear her; she didn't care—well, as long as he didn't come out of the house. It had been four months now, and Matilean couldn't hide it anymore. Her once-fitted clothes were making it obvious that something was wrong. She was a virgin before Seth—life just beginning, the world at her grasp.

"Oh, Mat, I knew you wouldn't understand. Daddy is old, and his way of thinkin' is old."

"You don't have to tell me. I heard'im."

"Well then, you should know you can't burst out with somethin' like that. It might kill'im. You got to wait til the right moment."

"I guess that wasn't the right moment, huh?" she scoffed.

"Mat, I'm serious."

"And so am I. Yo father don't even think he black. I mean, he might be light and even look white, but he just as black as me. Why he think like that?"

Seth was subjected to the belief that blood relationships firmly rooted his household and so many others similar to his complexion, and was never to be challenged. To mix with a person with a darker complexion was a violation of this belief. This was the first time Seth challenged the encumbered rules and boundaries that threatened his relationship with

Matilean. Seth understood that his father's beliefs could never be aggressively challenged. He also believed that Matilean was never subjected to such things; therefore, any confrontation with his father through her eyes would appear trivial. He knew now why he didn't explain his family's customs to Matilean when he had the chance. She would never understand that manhood did not provide a stronger incentive than upholding tradition.

"It's not his fault he thinks like that. He was trained to think like that by his parents, his parents' parents. It's forbidden, Mat."

"You right, Seth. I don't understand, but my stomach ain't gettin' no smaller. You think my momma gon understand? Just the other day she told me I didn't look right. Say my stomach gettin' bigger. Say I'm gainin' weight."

"And whatcha tell'er?"

"First, I told her somethin' was wrong with my period. I been bleeding for weeks. It made my stomach bloated. She said I'm gon bleed to death. Then she looks at me all-strange and she says, 'Ain't neva see no period make a gal gain dat much weight. You mus' thank I'm crazy.'"

Seth laughed, "And what you say then?"

"What could I say? She is crazy and she is right. It's like she know, but she waitin' on me to tell'er. Seth, my momma ain't dumb even though I tell'er dumb stuff. How long you think I'm gonna get away with that lie, huh? You know once my momma find out, I'm sure to be in the streets jus' like my sista Ruby. And Ruby messed with a dark man."

From the hedge, Seth plucked a small twig and placed it between his teeth. "Awe, hush Mat, yo sista Ruby ain't in no streets."

"Well, she was til my Aunt Bobby took her in. And Aunt Bobby got five kids, a no-good man and no more room, so who I'm gon live with? Sho can't live with you."

Matilean paused and waited for some type of reply.

Seth gave none. Instead, he continued to chew on the twig and glance at the passing cars.

"Seth... SETH! You listenin' to me?"

"Yeah, stop all that darn yellin'. I heah you. I told you, my father is old, and you heard'im. He'll die befo a dark person is ever allowed in the family."

"You mean dark or black, Seth?"

"Awe, you heard'im, Mat."

"So, Seth. Whatcha want me to do? Go up to him, like a slave to its master, 'Excuse me, Masa Woodson, Ah'm so sorry you old and half crazy, but Ah jus wanna apologize for endin' yo long tradition of excludin' dark-skinned blacks from yo blood line.' Is that what I'm suppose to do? How he gon exclude somebody black and he black. It's like he's usin' tradition to dilute the black blood out his bloodline. I don't know why, 'cause I gotta aunt who says if you got 1 percent of black blood in you then you black. She calls it the Virginia one drop rule."

"Well, Daddy's folks from Tennessee said it's always been 25 percent that declares you black. And Daddy says he got less than 12 percent in him, being that his parents are white and all. I heard a white man refer to Daddy as a Quadroon."

"You mean Coon, don'tcha?"

Seth let the twig drop. He bit on the back of his teeth.

"Who cares if he got 12 percent or 1 percent in'im, that nigga black!"

"All right, that's enough with the jokes, Mat."

"No, you need to stop with all the jokes. All I am to you is a big joke and everybody laughin'.

"Whatcha talkin' 'bout now?"

"I'm talkin' 'bout you. Yo daddy let the cat out the bag. You won't even gon tell me you was skippin' town on me. You don't care what's gon happen to me."

"I ain't skipping town on you."

"You goin' to vet-con, vet-lam."

"Vietnam, Mat."

"Well, wherever it is you goin'. I'll be heah by myself. And school just round the corner."

"I know all this, Mat. You ain't tellin' me nothin' new. I mean there's a lot on my mind, too—you being young, and Daddy and his thinkin'."

"You think this baby gonna care how old I am, what yo daddy think, or what color it is, whether it be light or dark, black or white, when it gets in this world? I'll tell you what color ita be, Seth. Ita be black, lookin' for someone to take care of it. Seth, I can't do this by myself."

She tried to calm herself. She didn't want to cry. Sometimes, once she got started, she could go on for hours. She backed off the gate, turned away from Seth, and sat on the top rock step. She raised her head to take a glance, and she saw Seth standing directly over her, blocking the sun's rays from her eyes.

"What?" she asked.

Seth didn't know it, but his words cut her like a knife. Sadly, she sat on the rock, confused and lonely. Seth placed his hand on her back. The gesture was comforting to her, but still she felt no assurance that everything would be all right. She was at their mercy and that hurt more than any malicious words they could say. All the strange signs, awful comments, and old traditions couldn't make her desert from her only chance of shelter.

2:10 p.m.
Saturday Afternoon

The days seemed to get shorter as Matilean's burdens weighed heavier. She once dreamt about the school dance, graduating, and college. Now, as she reflected, her fears were no longer molehills, but unmovable mountains. If she had been told that the direction of her life would be decided in the next two days, Matilean would have dismissed such notions.

She knew exactly what she expected from herself and her expectations did not resemble those of the neighborhood girls or the women surrounding her. Yet, she found herself in the same set of circumstances that birthed their reality: having a baby, then dropping out of school to support it.

The only thought in her head was that of her mother's voice saying, "You betta' stay away from dem wanna be white folks. Gal, they'll have you somewhere sinnin' or dead, and if you sinnin', you might as well be dead cause you'll be on yo way to hell."

Then it was the voice of Old Man Woodson, *"Ain't no dark person eva been in this family and it'll be ova my dead body if there eva is one."*

She did not hold to any of their warnings, which came to fruition the moment Matilean yielded to temptation and gave it the right of way to her life.

When Matilean pursued a desire to be wanted, she attracted temptation. The availability of a willing listener took her behind a twisted staircase to an old storage room underneath the auditorium. Everyday she and Seth met there and took advantage of an antique stage set and the eternal silence of a few decomposing wax figures that held their secret conversations and an act of fervor.

His seductive voice echoing off the old chipped paint drew her consciousness to his every touch. The wax figures observed the collapse of Matilean's will power as she felt the satisfaction of his sweet, pleasurable kiss, which consumed the fading knocks, screeches, and cracks found in the old storage room. There, in that deep, congested storage room, Matilean's virtue was lost.

Afterwards, she sat up and shamefully buried her face to keep the waxed smiles and frowns from convicting her of such sinful behavior. Without a sound, she slipped on her undergarments, adjusted her dress, and drew her legs back into her chest; then she shed tears of humiliation. Unwittingly, she uttered under her breath, "The wise shall inherit glory, but shame shall be the promotion of fools." It was a scripture her mother would quote verbatim when she suspected any of her children were committing sinful acts. Matilean felt she had committed the ultimate sin in the eyes of God and her being pregnant was surely her punishment.

Seth sat on one side of the rail as she sat on the other. He wasn't sure what he should say. Everything he said up to that point seemed to be wrong. Occasionally he observed her gazing face for an opportunity to break the silence. His tongue couldn't wait any longer.

"Whatcha thinkin' 'bout?"

Her eyes rolled over in his direction and then back. How could he ask such a stupid question? What else could she be thinking about?

Quickly, he apologized. "I didn't, I mean...."

"Stop, Seth," she spoke, "I'm thinkin' 'bout the things that brought me over heah, a baby, and where am I gon live and school. Too many things, Seth, for my mind to even process."

His head jolted toward the sky. What could he say that would comfort her? He knew no alternatives that would help the situation. The more he tried to think, the more it gave him a headache.

"I just need time to figure this out," he said.

"Time?" she asked cynically. "Time to go back and erase what happened? Time to listen to my mother and her prejudiced advice? Crazy as it sounds, it coulda protected me from all these heartaches, lies, sleepless nights, and a baby. Time is the one thing I don't have, Seth."

Already frustrated, Seth grudged, "You talk as if it's all my fault."

Matilean drifted along with one of the streaking clouds before saying, "No, I gotta take my share of the blame."

She turned towards him and asked, "Are you scared, Seth? Are you worried for me? Because one minute you wanna protect me, and the next you don't wanna accept me."

"It's not that I don't want to accept you."

"I get it, you don't wanna accept being a father. My momma said anybody can make a baby, but it takes a real man to be a father. Now I know what she means."

"Huh, yo mother, the great Christian, has spoken again," he said sarcastically. "She always tellin' you somin'. The truth of the matter, I'm scared of a lot of things: bein' a father, goin' to war, and my daddy. I never saw myself havin' no kid."

He dropped his head, studying a pattern in the sun-baked dirt. Such things relaxed him and allowed his words to flow smoothly.

"I don't know how to be a father. I don't know where to start." Seth smirked, "I guess I already started."

She cut his smirk short with razor sharp eyes. "You plantin' a seed don't make you no father."

"I know that and I don't want to run out on my responsibilities, but what I'm gon do? I'm leavin' fo boot camp on Sunday."

"What you're doing is constantly makin' excuses."

Some parts of him seemed to accept the fact he was leaving; it was as relieving as shifting his weight

from one foot to the other. He understood he had
a responsibility to stay, but on the other foot, who
would think he was being irresponsible because he
was going to war? A man called to war had to go,
simple as that. The responsibility of war and its real-
ism conjured fears that sank him deeper and deeper
into thought. He kept talking, oblivious to any of
Matilean's remarks.

"I don't know what's gon happen after I leave."

"At least you know where you're goin'," she
was quick to comment.

His eyes gave clarity to his thoughts of death.

"I don't even know if I'm gon make it back. I
read in the paper that thousands of kids my age are
dyin' every day over there."

"Why go?" her voice pleaded, and continued,
"why you got to fight that war when we got a war
goin' on right heah? Black folks havin' a hard time,
they already killed Malcolm X. And they still burning our churches, and you gon run off and fight their
war? Fo what? You ain't gon have more when you
get back. They gon make sure of that. Seth, I need
you heah with me."

His eyes continued to follow the dirt trail now
being traveled by various insects, and something
as minor as two ants fighting over a morsel of
food symbolized the war and death in his eyes. He
thought he would soon be just like those ants. From
his back pocket he pulled Thursday's newspaper.

On the front of the *Lynchburg Daily* was a large
headline that read, "Bodies Will Come and Bodies
Will Go" summarizing the fate of many innocent
young American boys that would be slaughtered for

no true cause. Underneath the picture, the caption read, *"U.S. planes begin combat missions over South Vietnam. Over 184,000 United States troops will have been committed to combat by the end of the year."*

Seth remembered the first time he saw something killed. He and several of the neighborhood boys hiked the local creek for tadpoles. It wasn't uncommon for them to hike for miles, but they usually stopped just before the slaughtering plant. They had heard of the legions of other boys their ages exploring too close to the factory and accidentally getting slaughtered—supposedly mistaken for one of the hogs.

It was Seth who suggested that they keep going. He had heard how the county hogs made good riding horses. The idea was innocent enough for a try. From the creek they approached the log fence that kept the hogs from getting out. The fascination of knuckling the pigs into the sloppy mud to fight for position momentarily numbed their sense of smell.

Although Seth was fascinated, the squealing that came from within the thin, tin walls of the factory moved him away from the others to a convenient hole that was cut out of the tin wall by rust and a continuous dripping of rainwater. He grew anxious and nervous. His right eye maneuvered around the hole until he saw one of the pigs sitting in a tub of boiling hot water.

Seth pressed his eye closer to the rusty hole, at one point laying his entire body against the tin to see what was happening. One man was holding another hog down, and another man walked up with a pistol in hand. The man holding the pig pulled a long knife

110

from behind his back and jabbed the blade into the pig's throat. The pig jerked hard and bucked as the blood spilled from its throat. But it was the gunshot to the animal's head that sent Seth into an all out sprint. Seth's running was warning enough for the boys to give chase. It scared him so to knowingly be in the face of death and unable to do anything about it. Until now, Seth had suppressed the entire incident.

Unconcealed fright latched to his realization of war because he knew that during war such situations are unavoidable. He slapped the paper with his fist and tossed it into the yard.

"You don't have to go," pleaded Matilean.

"Oh, God, I might not make it back!" He drifted back into consciousness. "Mat, what if I don't make it back?"

She gently placed her hand on his shoulder, "Do you wanna come back?"

"That's a stupid question!"

"No more stupid than you havin' those thoughts. If you wanna come back, then you'll make it back." She retreated with an utterance for a desperate solution to their problem. "The question is, will I be in yo plans when you get back?"

"Mat, sometimes it's hard for me to express how I feel, but I'm gon figure somethin' out."

His reply was sufficient for the moment.

"Seth, why go?"

"'Cause, I don't have a choice; I was drafted."

"So."

"So! If I don't go, I'll be put in jail, and I don't want to spend the rest of my life in jail."

"I feel like I'm in jail now," she whispered.

What was difficult for him to express was easy for her to see in his eyes; yet, it didn't prevent her from seeking a worthy explanation.

"My father served in World War II and his father before him fought for his country. So I'm supposed to be the first Woodson to coward out and run to another country like so many others? I gotta go. I gotta fight. I gotta show my father that I am a man. He expects me to."

"Seth, you can show'im you're a man by helpin' me. I need you just as much as that war."

"Listen, Mat, before I leave tomorrow everything will be resolved. I promise."

His response was intended for comfort—a promise to ease her mind and remove her uncertainties concerning the future for her and the baby. As he purposely kept from looking into her eyes, she knew it was doubtful that such words could accomplish their objective.

Somehow Matilean wished she could hide all of her troubles as easily as the sun hid itself behind a few of the passing clouds. She shut her eyes and helplessly drifted away in the shade that the clouds provided. It had captured her and temporarily removed all fears. She knew her troubles would inevitably arouse the curiosity of those around her. For the moment, she allowed herself to escape within the shadow of the clouds.

She closed her eyes, lifted her head towards the heavens, and inhaled the sunshine that lingered in the air. As she pretended to caress the heavens with her cheeks, she stretched out her arms and mocked a bird that soared to the endlessness of freedom, never returning to a place so full of racism, prejudices, and consequences.

She climbed high into the sky above the clouds, trying to skim the heavens in search of a haven. Even when the screen door slammed into the wall of the porch, she refused to let go of that solitude. She held on to it and the hope that some miracle would prevail and liberate her.

Was she too young to know or even realize that such an act of fervor would have such gravity? The thought of such gravity was swiftly dropping her from flight. Who would be there to break her fall, she wondered.

Matilean could hear several voices emanating from the porch. Afraid he might get exposed comforting Matilean, Seth jerked away, then quickly stood to his feet. His eyes showed relief when it wasn't his father.

Claudia, Victoria, and Ophelia, Seth's sisters, rushed onto the porch in hysteria. Even though they were cautious to mute their laughter with covered hands, a few giggles seeped from underneath their fingers.

"Shhhhh," Claudia insisted. "If you wake Daddy befo he goes to work tonight, he'll beat some black and blue on us."

The three girls danced around the porch in laughter until Claudia spotted Seth standing. She whispered in Ophelia and Victoria's ears. Again, the three covered their mouths to hold back their giggles. Each of the girls had distinct Irish cheekbones. One couldn't be certain if the genetics were from Mrs. Woodson or Old Man Woodson's side of the family, since rumor had it that the two were from the same bloodline.

Ophelia led the other two girls to the edge of the porch. Matilean heard rumors of Ophelia being undercover and sneaky. Ophelia fooled many with her fake, southern charm, which was quick to spill out an "I dos declare" or "Have mercy on me," during any conversation.

As often as possible, she swung her silky long hair that delicately flowed in layers like ocean waves over her velvet skin. She had on a pair of high shorts that exposed her long, reddish legs and knobby knees that resembled a flamingo. How she loved to prance around and strut, never yielding to any given order except Old Man Woodson's. Other than flaunting the fact that she was the prettiest of Old Man Woodson's children, she was equally delighted that Old Man Woodson's favoritism contested anyone who begged to differ.

Ophelia had a coldness that was well hidden. Often Matilean expressed to Seth that her eyes were too close together. Matilean spoke of her mother's sayings about people with close-set eyes. *"It was an evil that anca itself deep in a person's heart. 'Dem the ones you fear da' most cause they give the pearance of snow white, but the devil is a lurkin'."*

Claudia was sharp and jagged. With a coarse raspy voice that coincided with her rough appearance, Matilean believed she had to be as rough as the roughest man. She possessed features most similar to Old Man Woodson. Her face was structured like an inverted pyramid; she appeared to have a big forehead and little to no chin. A bad case of chicken-pox left scars that masked much of her beauty. Claudia's pleasure was the toughness she acquired from her father. Sure, Lillian pretended to be mean, but everyone in the neighborhood knew that Claudia was strong like an ox and to use another cliché, "as mean as a rattlesnake." Since Claudia was the oldest, and since Mrs. Woodson had long given up cooking and taken on drinking, she taught Claudia through years of practice how to assume the roles of a housewife: cooking, cleaning, and even outside chores.

Over the years, the manly chores developed Claudia's lean muscle definition, which pushed defiantly through her tough skin. She wore her hair in a mushroom bob, no makeup, and a pair of blue knickers that revealed her scarred knees that resulted from constant fighting.

With her arms gradually lowering, Matilean could feel their eyes stabbing her in the back. Before she could say anything, Seth was already shouting, "Don't come out here with none of that foolishness, you heah?"

Matilean made her way to her feet but refused to face her adversaries. There were more important things on her mind than them. She, however, listened with an inquisitive ear.

"Well, Brotha," cooed Ophelia. Sometimes those who knew Seth referred to him as Brother. Stylishly, with a dangled wrist, Ophelia pointed her index finger towards Seth. "Why on earth are you screaming at your siblings in such a tone of voice? Now, you don't want to give yo neighbors the impression you don't like us, do ya?" With one step, Ophelia covered a large portion of the porch. She held her chin high and with a patented extended neck, she sashayed back and forth along the porch.

"Are we embarrassing you, Brotha?" A derisive tone accompanied her question.

"Naw, but better you know, I don't feel like bein' the center of yo amusement."

"On the contrary, it isn't you that we find amusing," she snickered, then whisked her head around for affirmation from Claudia and Victoria.

"Maybe it's the way the sun has cast a shadow that doesn't match the frame of yo body," Claudia said hatefully.

As Matilean lowered her arms completely, she turned to face the girls. With sudden realization, Ophelia exploded with drama, "Well, Claudia, what on earth are you talking 'bout?" She looked towards the sky, then continued, "I dos declare, that's no shadow—that's Matilean."

The girls burst into uncontrolled laughter.

"Sugar, you need to get out of that sun or it's sure to ruin yo skin." She paused as having gained new insight. "Then again, you're dark enough to provide yo own shade."

Claudia was the first to attempt to contain the situation when it appeared that the only reply would be that of silence. In receding laughter, "That's enough, Ophelia."

If this was a test to see if Matilean would break and retaliate, it was affecting Seth more than her. His scrunched facial expression indicated how firmly he gripped the iron rail. Matilean placed her hand on his and gently squeezed, enabling him to reduce his temper and regain his composure.

Ophelia was Seth's fraternal twin but younger than Seth by two minutes, making Seth older than Victoria by twenty-five months and twenty-six minutes. The birth order was probably beneficial for Victoria since most of the badness that was being genetically passed around skipped her; however, Lillian and Biff received the remnants.

Matilean was not surprised to see Ophelia or Claudia on the porch making fun, but she was surprised to see Victoria. Victoria was a year older than Matilean, but Victoria had been held back a grade. The two girls had attended a few of the same classes. She knew that Victoria was sensitive, reserved in nature, and giving in spirit. She drew the conclusion that Victoria wasn't like any of her sisters. Matilean often thought she had to have been adopted.

Although Victoria was a Woodson, Matilean saw first hand how cruel Victoria's family treated her at times. Besides being slightly mentally challenged, Victoria's chubby size further provoked meanness from her siblings and friends. She had such a plump anterior and a rear to match that boys would often taunt by saying, "She was the wife of Mr. Potato Head."

Unlike Matilean, who often fought back with other attacking words, Victoria would admit defeat with a downpour of tears.

3:00 p.m.
Saturday Afternoon

Even though Ophelia had been given two or-
ders, she was reluctant to listen. She had a tendency
to push, and she would go on callously pushing the
fragile line of Seth's and Matilean's tolerance. Seth
was no immediate threat to her; only a lashing would
come from his tongue. Anything other had better be
as carefully chosen as a watermelon. Ophelia knew
that her daddy was her protector and he wouldn't
allow a hand or a word of anger to hurt his perfect
daffodil (unless, of course, he hurled it). That was
Ophelia's safety net. Seth and everyone on the porch
knew it, except for Matilean, who was about to re-
turn fire, when Seth ordered her to stop.

"But I ain't no shadow, Seth."

"I know, but let me handle this."

"Then handle it befo I do."

"Listen, all she wants is for you to say somethin' so Daddy will wake up, and we don't need that
trouble."

"I dos declare, Matilean, you don't have to wear
those old and dirty clothes. I just sent a box to the
Salvation Army," Ophelia added.

Matilean's soft face suddenly looked strained.
"My clothes may be old, but they ain't dirty. And it
ain't what you wear but what you know."

"From where I'm standing, you don't seem to
know too much—like comin' where ya not wanted."

Ophelia's attitude was encroaching upon Seth's
temper. She hated Seth for bringing this dark, black
girl into their personal lives to threaten what their

118

father was trying so hard to preserve for them. How dare he, she fretted.

She wanted to expose Matilean for what she thought Matilean was, a tramp—a Jezebel looking for someone to latch on to. She sought to break Seth by attacking Matilean. That motivated her resentment, the mother of her hatred. Ophelia's hatred was so deep that darkness and vengeance reflected in her eyes. She lazily spoke with no effort to disguise her malice.

"Do I detect a tempa from yo friend?" She hesitated, "Daddy always said some stray cats are good to keep, but I am sure he won't referring to alley cats. I tell ya, they're good for only one thing—having babies." She laughed. "If you can't control your pet then you need to take it back where you found it."

Claudia joined in with more brazen insults, "Seth, I thought Momma told you that if she can't use yo comb then don't bring her home."

Even though, Matilean frowned, her family supported those same sentiments.

"A comb get through that hair?" laughed Ophelia while adding, "she's part of the snappy, nappy from the no-comb tribe." Ophelia paused to think of a final insult that would piss Seth off. Then it came to her. "Well, I didn't know you were color blind Brotha, 'cause she definitely fails the brown paper bag test."

"Uh un', them fightin' words, Seth," Matilean murmured, before attempting to step towards the gate. Seth's nostrils began to flare; he had heard enough. He pulled Matilean back and headed towards the gate.

In this family there was a hierarchy that did not consider age or argument; Seth was third in the chain of command. Claudia and Victoria had wisely stepped away from Ophelia by the time Seth reached the porch. Ophelia backed away as he approached. She believed Seth wouldn't dare raise his hand to strike her, yet there was a speck of doubt that lingered in her throat. She swallowed hard when his eyes forced her into a corner of the porch.

A series of horn blasts caught Seth's attention. A white Cutlass convertible with wide, white-wall tires pulled up in front of Old Man Woodson's house. Seth gave Ophelia a long, intense stare before starting towards the car. Ophelia's brow puckered, then she burst into tears, "I'm telling Daddy," she blurted, then ran into the house. Claudia and Victoria ruptured into laughter. Matilean was disappointed that she had not given her something to really cry about.

PT Peterson popped his head from the car window. "Seth!" he screamed.

"PT, what have you gon and done now?" grinned Seth, as his eyes scanned the car from front to back, occasionally checking out his reflection in the clear shine the car gave off.

"I just drove it off the show room floor." PT smiled through every word.

PT had a soothing voice and an air that was smoother than the shine on his new car. He wore a brand new pair of burgundy penny loafers and creased khakis that he accessorized with his wavy hair.

"It has red bucket seats, power steering and brakes, tinted glass, console with tack, and simulated wire wheels."

"This car is loaded," replied Seth with excitement. "How did you get it?"

"I sauntered into Burley's Motors, ran my finger down the side. I had to get it. I simply asked Burley what he wanted for it. You should have seen him, Brother; he came from around his desk and paused to take a good look at me and put his arm around my shoulder." PT grabbed Seth's shoulder and wrapped his arm around him to escort him around the car.

"Then what?" asked Seth, who waited anxiously for the completion of the story.

"Then he says, 'Aren't you Sunny's boy?' Why, yes, sir, I answered politely and white like. Then he asked, 'How is yo daddy doing these days? I haven't seen him lately.' Oh he's fine, sir. Just fine. Of course, being considerably more polite like. 'And his business?' Before I could answer, he turned to a fellow salesman to tell him my father bought his first car from him. Sure did, I replied. Then he looked at me and said, 'I would have bet my house and my dog that your father was a white man the first time I met him.' I stared at him as if I didn't know my father looked white. Then I said, you don't say. And the other salesman looked at me and said, 'He looks white, too.' I smiled. Burley then asked, 'Son, you sure you have enough money for this car?' So then he introduced me to one of the loan officers who happened to be there browsing."

"You sure are good with those words, PT."

"Don't mistake it to be the words alone, Brother. It has just as much to do with who you know as it does with how you speak. My complexion just gave me an advantage to get through the door so I was able to meet the right people. Time is slow to change, so learn to use what you have to get what you want. That's my father's saying. Until we can change the system that's what we have to do."

That was the first time Seth actually thought of the benefits his complexion offered. Now he understood why his father was so adamant about keeping to tradition. Still, parts of him knew that someone had to be the agent of change. He wasn't sure if it would be him.

Matilean happened to be listening when PT gloried in his admission of looking Caucasian. She was concerned with whether Seth would volunteer or be coerced to go along with change. One way or the other, change is unavoidable. Both Seth and Matilean knew that.

Matilean stood near the gate and watched the two bask in the sunlight over the car's appearance. PT described the other features on the car and his descriptive words lured Claudia and Victoria from the porch. Claudia purposely bumped into Matilean as she exited the gate. With a slight grin, Victoria cordially apologized for Claudia's behavior.

"That sure is a pretty car, PT," remarked Claudia. "Take me and Victoria for a ride?"

"Sure, but not right now, later. I have some important news I want to tell your daddy."

"What? You gon ask to marry Ophelia, huh?" questioned Claudia, and then spitefully looked toward Matilean.

Wonder what she's tryin' to imply, thought Matilean. Immediately Matilean responded with a roll of her eyes. The thought of marriage then dawned on Matilean as an option to her dilemma, but she knew Seth wouldn't, nor couldn't marry her. Part of her was relieved knowing that he wouldn't ask.

Why would anyone in their right mind willingly want to be in this family anyway, she considered. She looked intently in their direction, but her mind was practically engulfed in the idea of marrying Seth. Matilean deliberated to herself. Is it even conceivable under the circumstances that he would ask? No, according to her family traditions, it was more customary for shotgun weddings to be encouraged by the bride's father. And such motivation was normally a double barrel pointed in the face of a soon-to-be son-in-law. She contemplated the scene with a glare. Somehow she and her tradition failed one another.

Finally Seth's waving hand came into focus, and Matilean stood alert for his direction.

"Come heah and see PT's car."

"Why?" she remarked, "ain't it big enough to see from heah?"

Claudia threw her head in Seth's path at the mere thought of allowing anyone to speak to him in such a way.

PT slapped his hands together in laughter. "That girl sure has a tongue on her. Who is she?"

"Oh, that's Matilean," Seth said nonchalantly, as he moseyed to the back of the vehicle, pretending to be more interested in the car than her disobedience.

His course of action was intended to divert PT from any further inquiries concerning Matilean. Matilean considered the demeanor of the well-dressed PT to be much like the luxury car—flashy, flirty, and fun. Matilean had only heard of PT once prior to his sudden appearance. She remembered Seth telling her stories about a cousin who courted Ophelia. She also remembered how grotesque it was to know such a thing and still persist on engaging in it. She used to doubt Seth's stories, but why would anyone fabricate a debauched story about their own family. She figured there had to be some truth to the matter.

PT fit the standard look it took to marry a Woodson: light complexion, straight hair, and, to top it off, his family had money. One thing Old Man Woodson liked better than a nearly white candidate was a rich, nearly white candidate. PT was a few years older than Seth, but that didn't concern Old Man Woodson as long as he didn't have to spend his own money for the wedding. The bride's father paying for the entire wedding was a tradition Old Man Woodson was more than willing to break.

Sure is a shame he's courting Ophelia, she contemplated. She offered a genuine smile as her salutation. "I apologize for sounding so rude," she added.

Claudia hastily replied, "What do you expect from those across the tracks?"

If Seth wouldn't demand respect then she would take the liberty of doing it for him.

"You're from the south side?" PT asked.

Tentatively, Matilean answered, "Yes, Capital Heights."

"Yeah! I know that area. I have lots of friends from over there. You wouldn't happen to know Bobby Tanner?"

Matilean smiled with confirmation, "You mean, Pretty Bobby?"

"That's him. I'm telling you, Seth, this boy should be a model or something. So pretty the women ask him for beauty secrets." He talked on, "How about Cookie Jones?"

"CJ? She's good friends with my sista."

Seth blurted, "How come you know so many people from ova there?"

"Half of them people are my father's customers."

PT's father was the only black florist in town. The majority of his business came from the funeral home due to an untimely death of a north-or south-side black. The majority of the families living across the south side of the tracks had a darker contrast to those few living across the north side of the tracks. This had nothing to do with longitude or latitude; rather, it was more of a deliberate attempt to isolate blacks from whites. But as more fair-skinned blacks began to move into white, working-class neighborhoods, streamlined attitudes and customs of blacks would frame and punctuate the interactions and accentuate the separation between fair-skinned blacks and darker-blacks.

Even though PT was pleasant and amusing, it upset Matilean to hear him categorize her people, his friends, and his father's customers as "them people." With considerable discontent, she wished to challenge PT and his comment; instead, she merely accepted her role and maintained silence.

From afar, Matilean noticed her reflection in the car. The height and width of her body as it was crammed into the height and width of the car door had no real resemblance to her own image. Somewhere in that dimension, she considered the rules of racism. However, the rules were not as easily distorted as her image. The rules were explicit, understood, and upheld by all, and taught to be upheld in threatening times by white people and both light-and dark-skinned black people.

After the four had relished over the vehicle, they all started back towards the house.

"Ophelia sure gon like this car," Victoria gestured, while patting the hood of the car.

"Victoria, don't put yo paws on the car, you gon ruin the shine," Seth said.

"I thought I saw Ophelia on the porch as I came down the street."

Claudia supplied PT with the missing link to Ophelia's sudden disappearance.

"You did, until Brotha ran her in the house."

PT glanced at Seth, "Let me guess, her mouth?" then laughed.

They had climbed the rock steps to the front gate when Claudia angrily asked, "How can you laugh, PT?"

"Easy, I am aware of your sister's mouth. I have told her time after time to refrain from smart comments." Quickly he turned to Seth before pushing the gate open. "It was a smart comment?"

Seth nodded towards PT while Claudia argued the opposite.

"But it wasn't directed to Brotha," Claudia snapped.

Victoria attempted to play the peaceful mediator, "But you can't blame Matilean."

Claudia swiftly turned to face Victoria, "Shut up, Victoria," she insisted. Then scowling, "Blood is thicka than water and don't you ever forget it."

Matilean watched as Victoria's eyes dropped at the tone of Claudia's voice. Then Claudia turned to Matilean, expecting Matilean to give the same response.

Matilean was determined to stand her ground so she fixed her eyes on Claudia and didn't blink. Claudia outweighed her by thirty pounds, but if victory is weighed according to one's heart, then Claudia was in for a fight. With audacity, Matilean aimed her sight directly into Claudia's eyes and the two locked in a standoff. If Matilean thought the issue was settled, Claudia didn't.

Victoria was stunned that Matilean had such courage to stand up to her sister; however, she wisely disguised her excitement in Claudia's presence. PT playfully acknowledged, "Ladies, ladies, all this beautiful scenery and you two would prefer to stare passionately into each other's eyes? I am truly impressed."

Seth assisted by stepping between the two.

"G'on in the house, Claudia," Seth ordered.

Before removing herself, Claudia smirked, it was then understood by Matilean that the confrontation wasn't over—just temporarily deterred.

"Come on, Victoria," she yelled, and then stomped past PT to head up the steps and into the house.

Matilean gave a bashful smile of gratitude to Victoria before she carried out her order. No sooner than they disappeared, she closed her eyes and took a deep breath and gently exhaled.

"Are you ok?" Seth asked.

"I'm ok."

PT interrupted, "That's enough excitement for one day. But there is always a cherry on top of the sundae. Speaking of Sunday, aren't you leaving then?"

"Yeah, I gotta be at Fort Dix, New Jersey, by Monday night."

"Well, Brotha, I wish you the best. Are you coming inside to hear the news?"

"In a minute, PT," replied Seth.

"Well, it's probably better if I wait until your daddy wakes up."

"PT, that's a wise decision."

PT jogged the steps to the porch and went in the house.

They waited until PT entered the house before drawing closer to the gate. She wished Seth would forget for a moment who he was and where he was and wrap his arms around her like he did in the old storage room. Instead, Seth reached over the gate and pulled her close. She could feel the iron wires press into her side.

"Are you gon hit me?" he asked, while pressing against the gate.

The wires were pressed deep enough against his chest and stomach that she could feel his body and still be considered at a safe distance.

"Why would I do that?" she asked curiously.

"I figure to release some of that built up anger."

"You think my anger extends to you or yo sistas?"

In order to satisfy her question, Seth agreed with both of her choices.

"No, Seth, it's your tradition that upsets me and the fact yo sistas would fight so hard to protect it. Why else would Claudia not like me? Why else would anyone in yo entire family not like me?"

She shook her head out of shame. His family and many like them would bemoan the loss of traditional values. Even though it was those same traditions that the white man used to crucify blacks, now blacks adopted them to crucify other blacks. One thing was certain; she was adamant not to willingly participate in such things.

"My momma says, 'If we's divided, then we's conquered.' Yet she supports division amongst white folks and between other blacks. When will we learn from what the white folk have done and from what they still doin' to all our people? I don't see the government stoppin' the KKK from beatin' and killin' us."

"Wow, where did that come from, Harriet Tubman?"

She placed her hand over her heart. "It came from here, Seth. I don't expect you to understand. The more I think about this black and white thing, I just get angry."

"Girl, you're a female Martin Luther King, Jr. Maybe he can recruit you."

"Maybe. Then again, I might have preferred Malcolm X since his approach got people to listen."

"Yeah, right."

"Seth, I rememba' when I first saw you. You was comin' down the hallway, walkin' proud, so distinguished. Someone might think you owned the school. And you was beautiful."

From perspective, society had yet to allow a man to be beautiful, so Seth blushed at the thought of him, a man, being considered beautiful.

"I couldn't stop myself from saying somethin' to you," she said.

Seth uttered, "Excuse me, but I approached you."

"Well, what you didn't know is I put myself in yo path to be approached. But it was our first conversation that convinced me that you was the one fo me. It had nothin' to do with yo skin tone or where you lived or how much money you had." She rubbed her hand along his cheekbone.

"During that entire conversation, Seth, you neva once mentioned tradition or what you couldn't do, just the goals you wanted to achieve. And you spoke of them with such passion. Anything that you desire to be, I wanna be a part of it, too."

"All this time I thought it was my curls."

Matilean didn't laugh. "Is everything a joke, Seth?"

"Mat, I don't have the answers. I'd be lying if I said I knew what tomorrow held. Yo guess is as good as mine."

"Then we have today. We need to take today to decide for tomorrow."

"Whatda you expect me to do, Mat?"

"I expect you to be a man. You can fight for yo country, surely you can fight for yo child. This problem just ain't goin' away."

"Yes it can."

"Huh?"

"This problem—it can go away."

"Whatcha saying, Seth?"

"I didn't wanna mention this, but...," he hesitated. He didn't know how she was going to react. "You know Mary Ann from school?"

"Not really."

"Naw, you wouldn't, she's an upper classman. Anyway, there is a doctor in West Virginia who can perform an operation to remove the...you know. I can fix it so you can see him. And don't worry 'bout the money or gettin' there. I will take care of that, too."

"Seth, I may be young, but I ain't stupid. I heard of that kind of thing. I heard it's dangerous."

"Ah, where you hear that from? Nothin' happened to Mary Ann."

"So!" Matilean pulled away from Seth. "Do you know what you askin' me to do?"

Seth scanned the parameters before lowering his voice to a whisper. "We're too young to be raisin' a kid. Didn't you say you ain't got no place to go?"

"Yeah, but."

"How can we support a baby if we can't support ourselves?"

"We try, Seth."

His hands flew in the air in agitation, "I wish it was that easy. I'm leavin' tomorrow. Damn, why you so stubborn?"

"My momma'd kill me if she found out I did somethin' like that."

"Don't tell yo momma 'cause I sure as hell ain't tellin' my daddy."

"And the church, Seth?"

"You don't even go to church."

"I've gon enough to know that what you want me to do is wrong."

She was stunned and taken aback by his proposal; she was even more shocked that Seth had it all planned out. She considered the act vicious; she studied him like she would a stranger.

"How can you ask me to do such a thing?" she asked, sniffling.

"Well, there is another alternative. How 'bout an adoption?"

She wiped her watering eyes before the tears could fall.

"What?"

"You know, an adoption. Once the baby is born you give it up to some mo folks to take care of it. I overheard Momma on the phone sayin' how my Aunt Kat gave up hers."

"Hers? She gave up more than one?"

"According to Momma."

"Why would she do that?"

"Who knows with Aunt Kat, she just as wild as a mustang. She likes for the cowboys to ride long and hard until she bucks them off," he laughed. "But she always likes for'em to get back on," he laughed again.

Matilean frowned and lamented the fact that Seth had reduced love to a mere physical act.

"Well hell, I don't know. I guess she won't ready for no kids," Seth assumed.

"That'll be impossible anyway."

"Why?"

"Cause my momma gon know. She always looks at me with her nose turned up, sniffin'. Honestly, she got a nose stronger than a hound dog. When

Ruby got pregnant, no lie, my momma sniffed her up and down and told her she was pregnant."

"She ain't sniffed you out yet?"

"Maybe my scent ain't as strong as Ruby's."

Seth grinned at the thought of Matilean's scent.

"Well, yo momma got a strong nose or yo sista got a strong odor."

"If I look anythin' like Ruby did when she got pregnant, then I'll be bigger than a house. I know she'll kick me out."

She paused for a second to look deep into Seth's eyes. "Seth, all I got is you."

The impression of reality came back into focus.

"Then we back to my first option. If I'm not heah to help you, then what can I possibly do?"

"Seth, I don't know."

"Then, what is there, Mat, except this?" Seth inhaled deeply through his nostrils. "I'm tryin' to help."

He tried to present to Matilean a stronger reality.

"You remember what you told me you dreamed of becomin'?"

"I wanna be a lawyer."

"Why?"

"Because," Matilean paused, "because I wanna fight to remove racism from this country."

"So, you ready to throw all your dreams away? Once you have this baby, it will never happen. You will never get a chance to be a lawyer. You too young, Mat. We too young. This doctor will give us both another chance. Do you want yo life back?"

He took hold of her hand, "Think about it, it will be like a new start, baby. I can see it in yo eyes, Mat, yo dream, and you don't want to lose it."

She felt coerced to entertain the thought of seeing the doctor in West Virginia. No matter how much she didn't agree, she saw no other alternative out of her predicament. In one breath, Seth had offered his only choice of support and taken her only hopes of security.

"Mat, I'm tryin' to do what's best for the both of us."

She took a deep breath and with her exhale came an uncontrollable flood of tears. She yanked her hand from his.

"You're doin' what's best for yoself," she said, while choking on tears, "and that's keepin' yo father from killin' you or from havin' a heart attack, which eva comes first."

"Trust me, Mat."

"I did and now I'm pregnant."

She respected his honesty and imagined that his suggestion to alleviate the problem had to be driven by fear. Because Seth had a way of lifting her spirits and an even harder way of dropping them, she questioned whether his reasons for getting rid of the baby lay with traditional responsibility or a diminished love for her. She did not want to entertain the idea of Seth not truly loving her, but deep within herself, questions of acidic proportion back washed from her stomach to her chest. Truly, he was the only thing she wanted to hold on to and the more she drew closer, the more she found herself being driven back. Why fuss and worry about what Old Man Woodson would say, Seth's contradictions reminded her often enough.

# ABOUT THE AUTHOR

David Woulf is a diligent writer who captivates readers through reality. His novel *As I Stood at the Gate* was recently released in paperback. A compilation of poetic works entitled *Rooted in Truth* is coming soon. Upcoming novels include *Black Men, Keep Your Vows* and *Consummated*.

To order your copy of *Southern Complexion* or other of David Woulf's trade-books, books on cd, and spoken word with music cd go to www.davidwoulf.net or your local bookstore.